NEW GUN

"Barjack," Happy said. "Do you know where them two Yankees went?"

"No," I said, "but I bet you're a fixing to tell me."

"Oh, yeah," he said. "Well, whenever you and Dingle come back in here, them two went walking down the street in the direction a the hotel, but ole Peester, he has been out on the sidewalk a watching, and when they come close to where he was standing, he called them over, and then he invited them into his office, and then they follered him in there."

"So Peester's a conferencing with Doyle and Batwing," I said.

"Yes sir," said Happy

"Watch them real close, Happy," I said. "Before this here day's up, each one of them bastards will be carrying at least one shooting iron with him, but they won't be showing."

"Do you think—"

"I ain't thinking," I said. "I know they'll be gunning for me."

Other *Leisure* books by Robert J. Conley:

THE GUNFIGHTER
BROKE LOOSE
BARJACK
BRASS
THE ACTOR
INCIDENT AT BUFFALO CROSSING
BACK TO MALACHI

No Need for a Gunfighter

Robert J. Conley

LEISURE BOOKS  NEW YORK CITY

A LEISURE BOOK®

November 2008

Published by

Dorchester Publishing Co., Inc.
200 Madison Avenue
New York, NY 10016

ISBN 10: 0-8439-6077-9
ISBN 13: 978-0-8439-6077-8

Printed in the United States of America.

10 9 8 7 6 5 4 3 2 1

No Need for a Gunfighter

Chapter One

It's been a while since you heared from me, and there's a pretty damn good reason for that. The reason is just on account of things had quieted down a pretty considerable in Asininity since the last time I told you about. They got plumb sissified, and that's for real. There just ain't been a damn thing to jaw about, and that's the gospel damn truth. Hell, I even begun to get fat and lazy, much as I hate to admit to it. You might recall that I had come to Asininity a few years back and had whipped a son of a bitch what had stole my boots and my hat and my gun, my special Merwin and Hulbert Company, .45-caliber, self-extracting revolver. I say I whipped him. Hell, I might a kilt him. I don't know. I never checked to find out. But what I done had damn sure impressed the hell out of ole Peester, the pettifogging bastard what was acting as mayor of the town, and he went and made me the town marshal.

It weren't long after that I arrested that Vance Benson for a killing he done right in Harvey's Hooch House with me right there a watching. Well, I tuck Vance and the four other Bensons to the town jail right then and there, and the upshot of it was that Vance got his neck stretched and the rest of them went to the pen for a long rest. They was guilty of rustling, and I proved it on them. But when they final got out, they come back to Asininity to kill me. I got ready for them with dynamite, and I blowed them up and half the town with them, but I blamed the blowing up on them, and that little episode made me a big hero. Our silly-ass schoolteacher, ole Dingle, he went and wrote a dime novel about me, and it got me something of a reputation. Then I rounded up the Marlin Gang and sent them up the river, and another writing fellow writ about that one.

After that, the ole Widowmaker, ole Herman Sly, he come to town really just for a rest, but me and him got all shot up together, and when we had healed up enough, we went after the bastards what done it to us. It was the Jaspers, and we wiped their ass out. Dingle loosened up his damn pen again on that one.

Course, I didn't remind you that I had tuck up with ole Bonnie Boodle, the big-ass bundle what run the Hooch House, and I had bought into the place eventual and shut down the other saloons in town. Then ole Lillian come to town, and she went and stoled my heart, and I got myself hitched and we had us a kid, but then things sure did change. She turned into a wild-assed, rip-roaring bitch, and I sure was fortunate that Sly had come to town, on account of he went and stoled Lillian from me, well, kind of with my permission, and then he settled down in Asininity. I went back to my sweet Bonnie. Well, now that kind of brings you up-to-date. Nothing much happened around our little town after that. At least, not for a while.

I was setting in the Hooch House one fine afternoon, a sipping from a tumbler of brown whiskey and nuzzling my sweet Bonnie, when that cheap-ass mouthpiece Peester come a walking in, and he come straight over to my table where I was at, and he dragged out a chair, but then he hesitated a bit, and looked down at me, and he said, "Do you mind if I sit down?"

"Set," I said.

He set down in the chair, and he tuck off his hat, and then he just kind of fumbled with it and stared down at the tabletop.

"Can we get you a drink, Mr. Mayor?" Bonnie said.

"Uh, no, thank you, Miss Boodle," he said. "I—

But I went and interrupted him by insisting that he have a little sip of something, and so he ordered some kind of sissy drink what I can't recall just what it was. I could see that he was some nervous-like as if he had something on his mind that he was a wanting to talk about but he was just a little bit skeered of bringing up the subject, whatever the hell it was. He sipped at that sissy drink he had, and final I decided to see just what the hell it was what was hung up there inside a his skull.

"Peester," I said, "what the hell did you come in here for? You never come in here just to get that cute little drink, now did you?"

"Well, no, Barjack," he said. "Not exactly. I—"

"Well, what then?" I said, kind of snarly, you know. "Come on. Out with it."

I tuck a slug out of my tumbler and then stared ole Peester right straight in the face. He fidgeted some, but then he opened up his mouth pretty soon.

"Well," he said, "I just wondered, rather, I should say, I've been wondering, how things are going for you these days."

I hugged on ole Bonnie and tuck me a good long drink, and then I grinned at the bastard. "Just how does it look like to you?" I said.

He returned my grin but kind of nervous-like, and then he said, "I just thought, you know, that things might have gotten just a little too tame for you around here."

"I'm doing just fine here," I said.

"It's been awful quiet around here," he said, "and you've always been a man of action."

Bonnie pulled my face down and mashed it into her big titties and kind of wiggled around a bit and said, "He sure is. You can say that again."

"We were, uh, talking about you in the town council meeting," Peester said.

"Oh, yeah," said I.

"Some of the men said they thought you might be moving on pretty soon."

"Moving on?"

"Well, yeah. I guess they meant because things were too quiet around here for you now. Thought you'd be craving some action, you know. Moving off to where the action is."

"Just where is that these days?" I asked, kind of smarty-alecky like.

"Well, I—"

"Listen here, Peester. I ain't going nowhere. I'm just as happy as a shit bird in a fresh pile of cow shit. I don't need to fight no more fights, and if you think that I need fighting to keep me from being bored, well, you're just dumber than I ever give you credit for before, and I've always give you credit for a fair amount of dumbness."

"Oh," he said, "well, I suppose that must have just been a rumor that someone started."

"I reckon so," I said.

"My Barjack is quite content here," Bonnie said. "He's setting in a tub of butter."

Well, ole Peester finished up his sissy drink and made his excuses and got up to leave, and I swear that I thought I seen him stagger just a little from that one pink pussy drink he had. I didn't give no more thought to what he had said, figuring that if someone had started such a damn dumb rumor that maybe the town council was just worrying about how in the hell they would ever be able to replace me, me being the famous goddamn gunfighting lawman that I was.

Just about then that crazy ole Lonnie the Geek, who weren't really so crazy 'til he'd had him too much to drink, commenced to hollering around. I knowed he'd get that way before too much longer, but I let him go on drinking as long as he had the cash on hand to pay for them drinks. But by this time I reckon he'd done spent all his cash on account of the way he was a yelling at ole Aubrey to pour him another one, and he was yelling about how he was good for it and he'd pay up later on down the road. Course Aubrey knowed better, and he was refusing to give the Geek any credit. 'Bout then the Geek hauled out his six-gun.

"'Scuse me, sweet hips," I said to Bonnie, and I pushed my chair back to stand up. I could see that I wasn't going to be able to ignore the situation no longer. Ole Happy Bonapart, my depitty, was a setting on his high stool perching place and holding his shotgun at the ready, but I didn't want him blasting away with that thing in the Hooch House as busy as it was at that time, so I give him a wave to let him know that he could just relax. I walked on over to the bar and was standing just behind ole Lonnie.

"Aubrey," I said, giving Aubrey a wink, "Aubrey, go on ahead and pour ole Lonnie here another drink. This one'll be on the house."

The Geek couldn't hardly believe his ears. He turned around to look at me, and I could see the deep and sincere appreciation in his face. Hell, I thought he was like to cry right then and there. I slapped him on the shoulder and said, "Lonnie, just turn on around and belly up to the bar there, and let ole Aubrey pour you a big one."

"Barjack," Lonnie blubbered, "That's the nicest thing you ever done for me."

"That's all right, Lonnie," I said, "just turn around there," and I kind of shoved him around just to help him get ready for his fresh drink. Then I slipped my ole Merwin and Hulbert out of the holster at my side, raised it up high over my head, and brung it down on top of the Geek's head like I was trying to crack a tough walnut. He made a little noise like "uf," and then his knees kind a buckled, and his head drooped, and he just kind a sank real slow down on his knees, and when his knees both rested on the rail, he just slid over sideways and looked kind a like a baby gone to sleep. I reached down and picked up his shooting iron, and I waved ole Happy on over.

He slipped off the edge of his high perch and dropped to the floor. Then he come a running like as if there was some kind a hurry, but of course, there weren't. The Geek was out about like a hunk of cold sausage. I handed Happy the confiscated six-gun, and I said, "Get someone to help you lug this dumb shit over to the jail and lock him up for the night at least."

"Sure thing, Barjack," Happy said.

Happy had a lot of experience at lugging drunks to the jail. Hell, he had even got me over there a few times whenever I had went and passed out in the

Hooch House, and I would wake up the next day laying on a cot in a jail cell, but only in my case, the cell door would be unlocked. Anyhow, while he was busy taking care of that little chore I give him, I went back over to my table and set back down to my glass of whiskey and my ample-bodied woman. She reached a arm around me and hugged me close to her.

"Barjack," she said, "you sure know how to handle things."

"Hell," I said, "there ain't nothing to it, wet lips."

Then she give me a smack with them big, red, wet lips, and I let her suck on my mouth for a spell before I pulled myself loose and picked up my tumbler, which was by this time getting pretty low on contents. I turned it up and emptied it and then held it up high for Aubrey to see. He was over to my table quick-like with my bottle, and he poured my tumbler full again. I lifted it up to take a drink, and Bonnie said, "Thanks, Aubrey."

In just a short while, ole Happy come back in, having done deposited his lifeless-like load in a jail cell. He went to his perch, but I waved him back over to my table. He come walking over and looked down at me and said, "Yeah?"

"Set down, Happy," I said. "Have a drink with us."

"You don't want me up on the stool watching the room no more?" he said.

"Happy," I said, making my voice sound as exasperated as I knowed how, "how come I always have to tell you something two or three times before you catch on to it? Did I just tell you to set down?"

"Well, yeah. You did."

"If I said for you to set down here with me and Bonnie, don't that mean that I don't want you setting over there?"

"Well, I guess."

"You can't be setting two different places at the same goddamn time, now, can you?"

"I reckon not," he said.

"Set down," I said.

He pulled out a chair and set, and I waved at ole Aubrey again. "Bring Happy some drinking whiskey," I said.

Aubrey brung it pretty quick, and Happy lifted the glass and tuck a drink. "Barjack?" he said.

"Whut?" I said.

"How come you to want me to come over here and set with you and drink whiskey instead of me setting over yonder watching the room for any sign of trouble?"

I leaned across the table with my head kind a close to Happy like I was fixing to tell him some deep, dark secret what I had in me, and he leaned over toward me to hear it the better.

"Happy," I said, in a kind of a whisper, "it just come to me that you done locked up the only real potentiable troublemaker what we had in here, and so there just ain't no more need for that kind of vigitance."

"Oh," he said. "Okay."

I tuck me another drink, and Happy tuck one, too. Ole Happy was the best depitty I ever had, and I would even go so far as to say that he was a pretty damn good friend, too. But he weren't too smart, and he could get on my nerves. I just couldn't help myself from picking on him now and then for his stupid questions and comments. But I tell you what. If it come to a fight, ole Happy would be right there beside me, and likely he would lend a hand that would have something serious to do with the outcome. I sure wouldn't want to have to get along without him no more.

I said "no more" on account of I did lose him once, and I told about it too. You might recall it. I was afeard that ole Bonnie was a planning to kill me, and I told Happy to shoot her dead if he seen her come up behind me looking mean, and he just up and left town. He told me later that he just couldn't bring hisself to shoot no woman, not even if it was to save my goddamn worthless life. Well, when I found out that he had run out on me in my hour of need, I swore that if I was ever to see him again, I would knock his block off, and sure enough, he come back to town later, and I did. Then I give him his job back.

And I ain't been sorry for that neither. Not once. Even after things had gone and quieted down in town, I sure wouldn't let him go. Why, you never know when trouble might come along, and if it ever did come along again, I sure wouldn't a wanted to have to face it without old Happy. Why, hell, I had even let ole Bonnie take him upstairs a time or two for a good ole-fashioned romp in the bed, and Bonnie had said that he was pretty good, even if that first time she had tuck him up there had been his first time of all.

Well, I was thinking about that, and it kind of got to me. I guess you know my meaning. I kind of nudged ole Bonnie, and I said, "What do you say we scoot on upstairs for a bit, sugar nipples?"

"What about Happy?" she said.

"Hell," I said, "I don't want him coming along. Just me and you is all."

"Oh," she said, "that ain't what I meant, and you know it. I mean, you just invited Happy to come and set with us, and now you want to leave him here all alone just by hisself. That ain't polite, is it?"

"Why, hell," I said, "I don't see nothing wrong with it. I got him a glass of whiskey, didn't I? And I tuck him off guard duty. He'll be all right." I turned to face Happy and raised my voice up some. "Won't you, Happy?"

"What?" he said.

"You'll be just fine setting here by your own self if me and Bonnie goes off for a spell, won't you?"

"Yeah," he said. "Sure."

"See there," I said to Bonnie, and I stood up and pulled on her arm, and she come with me. We walked over to the bottom of the stairs and commenced our way on up. I never bothered taking my glass with me, on account of I always kept a glass and a bottle up there in our room upstairs for just such special goddamned occasions. I was amusing myself by watching Bonnie's big titties bounce as we walked up the stairs. They sure did bounce nice, too. Course, she was dressed, but her titties was mostly uncovered on account of the low-cut front side of her dress. We reached the landing at the top of the stairs, and I just happened to turn my head a little, and I seen that goddamned Peester coming back in the place. I slowed down a little and watched him on account of it was unusual enough to have him come in once, but twice a day was just too damned unusual and in fact somewhat by God remarkable.

"Looky there, Bonnie," I said.

"What?"

"Look it what just come in," I said.

She looked, and she said, "Peester?"

"Yeah," I said.

She give a shrug of her shoulders and her tits shrugged along with them. "So what?" she said.

"That makes twice in one day," I said.

"Oh," she said, "don't pay him no never mind. We got things to do, honey pants."

She had of late developed the bad habit of referring to me by them insinuating names. I don't have no idee where she come up with that bad habit.

Chapter Two

Anyhow I stepped back to where I could be out of sight of them downstairs but I could still sort a see them, and I said, "Hold on just a minute now, darlin' ass. I'll be right with you." I could see ole Peester go on over to my table where Happy was setting by hisself, and I heared him say, "I need to see Barjack." I was hoping that ole Happy would say, "You just seen him," but he never. Instead he said, "He ain't here just now, Mr. Mayor." Peester, kind a huffy then, said, "Where is he?" Ole Happy, he kind a glanced toward the stairs, and he said, "I don't think you want to see him just now. He's, well, he's a bit busy." Peester straightened hisself up as most he could, and then he said, "What's he doing?" Now I had to hang around to hear what ole Happy would say to that, and what he said was, "Well, Your Mayorness, he's went upstairs with Miss Bonnie, you know. Now I never asked them how come they was going up there, but I got me a pretty good idea, and it ain't something that polite folks talks about. I reckon you take my meaning?"

Bonnie was a tugging on my arm, and I was about to laugh right out loud. I couldn't have that, so I let her pull me on down the hall to the door to our own private little room, and I went inside with her. It weren't long before we was both just as nekkid as a mole out a his hole, and then, well, like ole Happy had said to Peester, what come after that, polite folks just don't talk about. But we did have ourselfs a right sweet time up there. I can tell you that much all right.

When we was final all done with our pleasuring, we laid around kind a fondling on each other 'til we had most recovered from all that adventuresome romping around, and then we got ourselfs dressed again and went on back down the stairs to our busy house of business. And business was doing pretty damn good. That's for sure. I led ole Bonnie right back to our table, and my whiskey glass was still a setting right there right exact where I had left it. We set back down, and I picked up my glass, and I asked ole Happy, "Didn't nobody spit in this while I was gone, did they?"

"Hell, no, Barjack," he said, taking my question real serious-like, "you know I wouldn't let no one mess with your whiskey."

I tuck a big slug from out a the tumbler and set it back down. "Just checking is all," I said.

"Mr. Peester come in here a looking for you while you was, uh, while you was out," Happy said.

"What did the paper-pushing, silly-ass little son of a bitch have to say?" I asked.

"He just said that he needed to see you was all," Happy answered me. "He wouldn't tell me no more."

Just then ole Widowmaker come walking in the front door. He stopped and looked the room over 'til he seed me, and then he come a walking right straight on over to my table. There had been a time when if the Widowmaker walked into a room it got real quiet, but ole Sly had been a living in our town now for a spell, and folks had just kind a got used to having him around. I was surprised though, on account of ever since he had got his ass hitched to ole Lillian, he didn't seem to have too much free time on his hands no more. It was pretty damned unusual for him to just come a wandering into the Hooch House any more. To tell you the whole damned truth a the matter, I just about had me a heart attack or something worrying about had he come to tell me that things wasn't working out between him and Lillian after all. But that weren't it at all.

Like I said, he come straight to my table, and the first thing he done was he tipped his hat to ole Bonnie, and he said a kindly howdy to her. Then he howdied me, and I said, "Set your ass down, Herman," and he did. "You come to have a drink with me, did you?" I asked him.

"Not exactly, Barjack," he said, "but I guess one wouldn't hurt me any."

I waved at ole Aubrey, and he brung Sly a drink right away. Sly lifted his glass like for a toast, and I picked up my tumbler and held it up high too.

"Here's to you, old pard," I said.

"And to you," said Sly, and we both of us drank some of our wonderful stuff. Bonnie and Happy tuck part in that little celebration too. Sly set his glass down and looked at me hard. I could tell he had something right serious on his mind.

"Happy," I said, "why don't you take up your perch over yonder again for a spell?"

He give a kind a funny look, but he picked up his shotgun and stood up. "Okay, Barjack," he said.

Then I tipped up my tumbler and emptied it out into my guts, and I shoved it over to Bonnie, and I said, "Sweet tits, take this over to the bar and get it refilled for me." She stood up and tuck my glass and headed for the bar. Then I give ole Sly a look.

"Well," I said, "what is it, ole pard?"

Sly leaned in toward me and said in a right low voice, "Barjack, I just had a visit from Peester."

"That's interesting," I said. "I had two just today. What'd he say to you?"

"He asked me if I would like to have your job," said Sly.

Well, I was really tuck back by that. I might even say that I was damn near shocked somewhat to hear it. I was stunned so that I couldn't say a damn thing for a little spell. I couldn't think of what to say. Ain't nothing that had startled me more since that time ole Bonnie had pitched me headlong down the stairs and I had learnt to fly. Bonnie come back with my drink and set it down. She could see that the conversation had turned sort of serious, and so she hesitated, but I shoved her chair back and patted it on the seat, and she went ahead and set down. My voice come back to me about then.

"Did he say how come my job might be about to come open?" I asked Sly.

Sly give a look to Bonnie, but I said, "Oh, it's all right," so he went on ahead.

"I asked him about that," he said. "He just told me that he thought it was about time you gave it up. That's all he would say."

I tuck me a drink, set the tumbler down, and scratched my unshaved cheek. I glanced at Bonnie, and she give me a worried look and said, "Barjack?"

"Never mind, honeypot," I said. Then I looked back at Sly. "What did you say to him about all that shit?" I asked him.

"I told him I wasn't interested," Sly said. "I'm no lawman, and I don't need the money."

"Something's up," I said, like as if I was in deep

thought. "That sly little bastard is up to something no damn good, and that's for sure."

"Barjack?" said Sly.

"Whut?" I said.

"Maybe I should keep my opinion to myself, but—"

"If you got any opinion on this at all," I said, "you just go right on ahead and mouth it."

If I had any friend at all in the whole wide world besides my sweet-ass Bonnie and good ole Happy Bonapart, it was the goddamned Widowmaker. Me and him had drunk some brown whiskey together, we had been shot all to shit together and mended up, and we had rid a long, hard trail in pursuit of them goddamned Jaspers together, and by God, between me and him, we had kilt the whole shitting bunch. We had done all that together. He for sure was the last fellow on the whole entire earth who had to be worrying about butting into my affairs.

"Well," he said, "I could be wrong, but I'll tell you what it looks like to me."

"Go right on ahead," I said.

"Barjack, it looks to me like Asininity thinks it has outgrown you."

"Just what the hell does that mean?" I said.

"When you came here it was a wild town, right?"

"Damn right."

"And you tamed it down. But then, you had the Bensons coming in, and after that we had the Jaspers to deal with. Right?"

"Well, of course. You know that. So what?"

"Things have been real tame around here since then," Sly said, "and on top of that, Dingle and that other writer have written several dime novels about what a wild, tough, gunfighting son of a bitch you are."

"Well, yeah, I said. "That's all true enough, but—"

"I think," he said, "that Peester and probably the whole town council have come to look on you as unnecessary and even as something of an embarrassment. They're trying to come up with some way of getting rid of you. Peester approached me, thinking that if they were to get rid of you some way and hire me in your place, I could take care of you for them—in case you objected."

"You mean, they figured you'd blow my ass all the way to hell for them?" I said.

"That's about what it looks like to me," Sly said.

"Well, that no-good, dilly-dally, three-cent, pettifogging, son-of-a-bitching shit ass," I said. "I'll knock his fucking block off. I'll—"

"I don't think you should do that, Barjack," Sly said.

"Then I'll do it," said Bonnie. "I'll whip his goddamn ass."

"Calm down now," said Sly. "Both of you. Now that you know what he's up to, you can take some time and think about it. Figure out how to deal with it quietly and legally. You don't want to do anything that will get the county sheriff after you. Beating up the mayor would be just a little bit stupid, don't you think?"

"I reckon you're right about that, Sly," I said, "but it would goddamn sure be satisfying."

Sly finished up his drink, and then he said, "All right. Stay calm and think about it. I'll back you up, Barjack. Any way that's legal. You just let me know. Okay?"

"Okay, pard. I'll do her. Don't worry about me none."

"I'd best be getting back home now," Sly said, and he stood up and put his hat on his head. "Keep me informed."

He left on out of there, and I could feel my old wrinkly face a burning red with pure-dee hate and bloodred anger. I'm surprised that all that burning never burned away all them wrinkles, but it never. That pettifogging bastard was trying to take everything away from me, all that I had worked so hard for so many years to build up: my job and the salary what come with it, the respect of the whole damned community, even my business what I had on the side. Now, you might ask how come would taking away my marshaling job take away the Hooch House also. Well, I'll tell you. As town marshal I had closed up all the other saloons in town. If my marshaling job was tuck away from me, why, there wouldn't be no way of keeping them other competing houses from opening right on back up. Then I wouldn't have no mono—what you call it—no corner on the market no more.

Now, I couldn't have that. There wasn't no way. I made up my mind right then and there, in spite of the advice that ole Sly had give me, that if it come to that, I would go out in a goddamned, rip-roaring, fourth of July blue-blazing battle the likes of which Asininity hadn't never seen before. I sure as hell wasn't going to resign and just go away quiet-like. Bonnie said, "Barjack? What are you going to do?"

"I ain't going to quit my job," I said. "That's for goddamn sure and certain."

"What if they fire you?" she asked me.

Well, that thought set me back. I had been thinking that they was going to try to make me resign. It hadn't really come into my head that they would dare to fire my ass. I didn't think that they would.

"Hell, Bonnie," I said, "they're too chickenshit for that. Do you think for even one single minute or even second that ole Peester would ever have the guts to look me in the face and tell me that my ass is fired?"

"Well—"

"Well, hell no, he wouldn't. If I was to bark at him, he'd curl up in a corner and cry. That's what he'd do. That's all he'd do, too."

"Barjack," she said, "I'm worried."

"Well, don't be, sweet butt," I said. "Don't you worry your pretty little head even the slightest wee little bit. I ain't going nowhere. Hell, I'm here to stay. You and me are here to stay. And what's more, we'll be right here in the ole Hooch House long after that pettifogger Peester is gone."

"But Barjack—"

"Now listen here," I said, "you heared ole Sly, didn't you?"

"Yes."

"The only way ole Peester would dare to fire my ass is if Sly would take my job, and then they figger that Sly would gun me down, and they'd be setting in high clover. But Sly ain't going to do that. They didn't figure on me and him being such good friends. Without Sly on their side, what the hell can they do? Huh?"

Bonnie kind a rubbed on my arm and snuggled up against me, and she said, "Well, I reckon they can't do nothing then."

"You're right about that," I said, and I drunk down the rest of my drink. I held up my tumbler for ole Aubrey to see, and he seed it and come a running with my bottle to fill it back up.

"Barjack?" Bonnie said.

"Whut, sweet pants?" I said.

"You remember back when Sly first rode into town?"

"Well, sure I remember. What about it?"

"You remember how it was that near ever'one in town thought he had come into town to kill them? They was all feeling guilty about something they had done years back. Remember?"

"Well, sure I remember." I give a little laugh. "I even thought for a little bit there that he might've come after me."

"And who else thought that?" she said.

"What the hell are you getting at, Bonnie?" I said. I never was one for playing no word games, and I had done had enough of this one.

"Peester," she said.

"That son of a bitch," I said.

"Peester thought the Widowmaker had come for him, didn't he?"

Well, now, my brain was a working overtime at figgering something out. It was just about to make some sense, but it wasn't yet quite coming together. Bonnie had a sly little grin on her fat face, and it was irritating me on account of I didn't have no idee of what she was a getting at.

"Him and half the rest of the town," I said. "I don't see how—"

"Barjack," she said.

"Whut?" I snapped back at her.

"Barjack, how come ole Peester to think that the Widowmaker was coming after him? Do you recall that?"

"Well, now," I said, scratching my head, "let me recall. It seems that ole Peester'd had some doings with—"

"With ole Singletree's wife," she said, her face just glowing with gleefulness.

"Or with ole Singletree hisself," I said, beaming up some my own self.

"That's right," she said. "Now just what do you think ole Peester would say to you if you was to say to him that if you was to get fired, that old story would get all around town?"

"And even all around the whole by God county," I said. "And prob'ly the second story more than the first one." I commenced to roaring with laughter, and Bonnie roared right along with me.

"Peester and Singletree," she roared in between her laughing.

Well, finally we sort of calmed down a little bit, and I tuck me a big swaller of good, brown whiskey, and I set down my glass again, and then I set up straight and got me a real serious look on my old face, and I said, "First thing come morning, I'm going right on over to ole Peester's office and have myself a good, long, serious talk with that pettifogging bastard."

Chapter Three

Well, it was damn near a miracle, but ole Bonnie was up and awake before me the next morning, and she had done ordered up a goddamn tub full of hot water with all kinds of bubbly shit in it, and then she shuck me damn near to death, but it woke me up good, and she made me get in that tub. First thing in the damn morning! She did have some hot coffee sent up to the room, and I slurped on that whilst she scrubbed on me with a long-handled brush. And she did scrub me too, all over, I mean. Whenever she was all did with me that way, she brung me a mirror and a razor, and she rubbed shaving soap all over my face and made me shave, and then final she tole me to get out and she tuck up a great big towel and rubbed me 'til I was dry and then some. Then I noticed my good suit a clothes a hanging on the wall all ready for me to get dressed up in. I guess she was real worried about my job.

I started to fuss about the suit. I thought that was going just a little too far, but when I seen the look on her face, all worried-like and all concerned about what was maybe about to happen, I just kept my face shut, and I went and started to climbing into that damned rig. Well, I got all dressed up in that black, three-piece suit and a clean white shirt and string tie and all, and I went for my boots and seen that they was shined up like as if they was brand-new.

"Bonnie, darling sweet tits," I said, holding up one of the boots, "you damn sure went all out, now didn't you?"

She set her big ass down on the bed right beside me and give me a look, and I thought I had saw every possible expression on her face, but I sure as hell never seen what I seen just then. It was worry, I guess. She was looking me right in the eyes.

"Barjack," she said, "I want you to be careful this morning. Be nice to ole Peester now. Don't hit him or nothing like that."

"Now, sugar boobs," I said, "we talked this all out last night. I got him right where I want him with that Singletree story. I don't need to kiss his goddamned ass."

"We think you got him with that," she said, "but we was drunk last night. What if he don't scare as much as we think he will? Don't take no chances, Barjack. Try not to piss him off."

"Humph," I snorted. "I think he's done pissed off already. I think it's a bit late to go worrying about pissing him off at this here late date. I think—"

"Barjack!" she snapped at me. "Promise me!"

And so I did. I really did swear my solemn oath that I would be nice and stay calm and would not do nothing calculated to piss off ole Peester, and then I strapped on my faithful ole Merwin and Hulbert Company .45 and put the hat on my head and started out the door. On my way down the stairs it come to me that I was damned hungry, so I stopped at the bar and tole ole Aubrey to have me a big breakfast whopped up and brung out. Bonnie never knowed about this pause in my progress toward ole Peester, on account of I'm damn near certain that just as soon as she seed me out the door and had extracted that there promise out of me, she went right on back to sleep.

Well, I set down in my favorite chair at my favorite table and waited on my breakfast, and here come ole Happy. He seed me and set down with me, and Aubrey called out to him did he want his usual breakfast, and Happy allowed as how he did. But I seed Happy just a staring at me with a kind a funny look on his face.

"What the hell's bothering you?" I final said.

He shuck his head a little bit and said, "Oh, nothing, Barjack."

"Happy," I said, "I'm going to kick your ass across the street if you keep on lying to me like that."

"I was just kind of wondering how come you was all dressed up the way you are," he said.

I changed my tune then, and I said, "Happy, ole Bonnie done this to me."

"She did?"

"She damn sure did. You see, I'm fixing to go see ole Peester, the goddamned pettifogger, and—"

"Barjack," Happy said, interrupting me, which I hate, "what's a pettifogger?"

"What's a—Hell, you ignorant shit. It's a—Well, it's a goddamned shyster lawyer. That's what it is. Now what the hell was I saying?"

"You was saying that you're a fixing to go see Mr. Peester, that goddamned pettifogger, and—"

"—and she don't want me whomping up on him none. She wants me to make a good impression and act nice and all."

"Oh," he said.

Just then ole Aubrey brung out our meals, and we commenced to wolfing them down. It didn't take too long to finish them neither, and then Aubrey, he filled up our coffee cups again. As I was taking a good slurp of that hot liquid shit, ole Happy said, "Barjack?"

"Whut?" I said.

"Barjack, has you got some kind of a problem with ole Peester?"

"Peester's wanting to get rid of me," I said. "I thought you knowed. I thought everyone knowed."

"I never knowed that," Happy said, so I went and tole him the whole story even including what ole Sly had tole me and even the almost-secret in ole Peester's life what was the reason he was so skeered when Sly had first showed up in Asininity.

"Well, I be god-diddle-damned," he said.

Well, I shoved my chair back just then and stood up. "I can't see no reason for putting this off no longer," I said.

"You going to kill him?" Happy asked.

"No, hell, Happy, I ain't going to kill him," I said. "Hell, didn't I just tell you I had to make a solemn oath to ole Bonnie that I wouldn't even hit him? I wouldn't even call him no bad names?"

"Well, yeah, but—"

"Hell, I'm the damn marshal. I can't go around killing folks. I'm just going over there to have me a little talk with him. That's all."

"Oh. All right then."

"All right?" I said.

"I just meant that if you was going out to kill someone maybe I should ought to go along with you, but if you ain't, I'll just stay here."

"That's fine, Happy," I said.

"Unless you want I should go over to the office," he said.

"You stay right here," I said, and I headed for the door. Behind my back I heared him say, "Yes, sir, I'll just hang around right here 'til you get back."

I stepped out the front door and stood there on the board sidewalk for a space just looking over the street. It was early yet, and there weren't much traffic on the street. A couple of cowboys rid up in front of Maudie's eating house and hitched up and went inside. I seed Howie down at the end of the street opening up the depot, and then I seed Sly a walking ole Lillian to her fancy-ass White Owl Supper Club. They seed me, too, and ole Sly, he give me a wave, and Lillian, all she done was just nod her head real kind of slightly-like, you know. I waved back at Sly. There was a few more, but I don't recall just now just who the hell they was. I tuck a cee-gar out of my pocket and struck a match and lit it on up. I got my cee-gar going real well, and then I commenced to strolling on down the street real casual-like on my way down to ole Peester's office.

Peester was just coming around the corner on his way to unlock his office door, and he seed me over his shoulder. He unlocked the door and then straightened his ass up and turned around to face me. I never hurried my step along. I just kept a strolling 'til I got up close to him, and then I said, real polite-like, "Morning, Mr. Peester."

He looked like as if he had been slapped across the face, but he forced a grin, and he responded a bit nervously to my greeting. "You, uh, you want to come in?" he said.

I walked in ahead of him, saying, "I come over to see you on account of I heared you was wanting to have a talk with me. What you got on your mind, Mr. Mayor?"

I just walked on in to his main office and tuck me a chair and flipped some ashes on his clean-swept floor. He give them a look, but he never said nothing. He walked on back behind his great big desk and sat down in his plush, red office chair. Then he leaned back looking real pompous-like.

"Barjack," he said. "You have your own business here in town. You've got plenty of money. You don't need to keep working as hard as you have been. It's about time you considered going into retirement. You could have an easy life. Relax. Let someone else, some younger man, take on all the responsibility and take the risks. Do you follow my meaning? I'm thinking about your welfare."

"Well, Mr. Mayor," I said, "I'm thinking about my welfare, and my thinking don't run along the same lines as yours. My thinking tells me that things is just fine the way they are. I got no complaints. None at all. So unless you got something else to talk to me about, I'll just be on my way back on over to the Hooch House."

I got up and turned to walk out, and old Peester, he stopped me.

"Barjack," he said. I turned back around. "Won't you reconsider?"

"I don't see nothing to reconsider about," I said. I tipped my hat to him and walked right on out his office, and I was thinking that if that was all he had to say everyone was sure making a big pile of shit out of just one little turd. I made my way back to the Hooch House, which was still official called Harvey's Hooch House, no one had ever changed the name, and no one could remember just who the hell ole Harvey was, and I went inside and back to my table and set down. There was one ole boy a standing at the bar a drinking. It was still early. Bonnie weren't nowhere in sight, and I was sure she was upstairs sawing logs like a portable sawmill.

"Coffee or—"

I never let ole Aubrey finish what he was a fixing to say. I just hollered out, "Brown whiskey."

He brung it over to me right quick. Happy was still setting there right where he was at whenever I had left out of there.

"That didn't take very long," he said.

"Hell no," I said. "He just asked me did I want to retire and I told him hell no and that was that."

"You never even said nothing mean to him nor called him no names?" Happy asked.

"I was just as sweet and polite as I knowed how to be," I said. "I even called his fucking honor Mr. Mayor."

"And that's all?"

"That's all. Well, I did kind of drop some cee-gar ashes on his shiny mopped floor."

Happy picked up his coffee cup and started in to take a sip, but then he looked at my whiskey tumbler and set his cup back down. "I think that this here calls for a drink," he said. He looked at me like he was my pet dog, and he added, "Don't it?"

"Sure, it does, Happy," I said, and I waved at ole Aubrey, and he brung Happy a drink. Happy held it up toward me, and then he tuck a big gulp of it. I had me a slurp of mine, and then I seen ole Bonnie come a flouncing down the stairs, her great big tits a bouncing up and down like as if they was going somewheres on their own. It was still some early for ole Bonnie to be up and around, and then I knowed for sure that she had been more than a little anxious about me. She got to the bottom of the stairs and come running straight at me. She never set down. She just leaned over and throwed her arms around my neck and damn near smothered me to death with her huge titties.

"Oh, Barjack," she said. "Is everything all right? You done been to see Peester? What'd he say? What'd you do? You never hurt him or nothing like that. Did you? You didn't cuss him out nor call him no bad names?"

I kind a tugged on her arms to get me a loose so I could breathe, and when I final did get me loose, I said, "Set down, Bonnie."

She pulled out her chair and set her broad but luscious ass down in it, and she said, "Well?"

"Well, Bonnie, my sweet little Boodle," I said, "I went to ole Peester's office, and all he done was just asked me if I didn't want to retire and just live off a my business interests here in Asininity and take life easy, and I told him hell no I didn't have no such intention of doing that, and then I left and come right straight back on over here. That's all."

"That's it?" she said.

"That's the whole damned story," I said.

"Barjack never even called him a pettifogger," said Happy.

"Well," said Bonnie, "that's it then. There wasn't really nothing to it. Was there?"

"I don't reckon there never was," I said.

Well, Bonnie went and ordered herself a drink and Aubrey brung it over, and the three of us was just a setting there and feeling good. I admit to being just a little bit disgusted with myself on account of I had been so damn nice to Peester when I really felt like tossing him out in the middle of the street headfirst and then rolling him around in the dirt just a little bit, but I decided that I could live with that, and besides, there would always be another chance. I tuck myself a good long swaller.

"It's a good thing Peester was nice to you," Bonnie said.

"Whut?" I said.

"I thought you was worried about Barjack being nice to Peester," Happy said.

"Well, I was that," Bonnie said, "but then, if Peester hadn't a been nice to Barjack, I would've whipped his ass real good for him. I can tell you that. I don't let no one talk mean to my Barjack."

"Just only your own self, huh?" I said.

"Now just what the hell do you mean by that?" Bonnie said.

"Why, nothing, sweet swishing hips," I said. "Not a damn thing."

"Well, anyhow," she said, "everything's just fine, and any trouble that might a been coming is done gone."

"Maybe," said ole Aubrey. He was at the front of the place a looking out the door onto the street. Ole Aubrey was damn quiet, but I knowed that he heared ever word what was said within a mile of him. He tuck it all in and mulled it all over. He was so quiet that no one of us had even noticed that he had come out from behind the bar and went to the front door, but there he was, and he had said that. Well, it sounded so omnimous-like, that the rest of us just got real quiet-like for a spell. We all looked at ole Aubrey. He was just a standing there staring out at the street.

"Whut?" I final said.

"What do you mean, Aubrey?" Bonnie said.

"Maybe everything's fine," he said.

"What do you mean by that maybe?" I said, and I come up out of my chair and headed for him. I felt like as if he was threatening my very happiness. "What do you mean?"

"Just what I said. I just seen Peester hurrying down the street like his house was on fire or something."

I squeezed myself up against Aubrey and craned my neck looking out the front door. "Where?" I said. "Where'd the son of a bitch go?"

Aubrey kind of nodded his head, and I tried to foller his nod with my gaze. "He headed into the bank," Aubrey said.

"Oh," I said, "is that all?"

Just then Peester come out a the bank, and ole Markham was with him, and they went to hustling down the street together. Me and Aubrey stared after them, and Bonnie and Happy come over to stand by us and watch.

"They're headed for the dry goods store," said Happy.

"For Chester Filbert," said Bonnie.

"They're a fixing to have a goddamn town council meeting," I said, the seriousness of the situation a settling in on me like a stack a bad flapjacks. "The sons of bitches are after my ass for damn sure."

Chapter Four

We stood there at the door and watched while ole Peester gathered up the whole damn town council, and they all walked with him back down to his office and went on inside to have their meeting. Well, I was sure getting hot, I can tell you that. Then I turned around and walked real slow back to my chair at my favorite table where my tumbler full of whiskey was setting there waiting for me. I was thinking about how good I had it there in Asininity and what all ole Peester was a planning to take away from me: my marshaling job, my business, my Bonnie, all my good whiskey, everything what I owned, what I had earned over all them years by all my hard and honest work. It was burning my ass, and that's for sure.

I set back down and tuck me a long drink. I was trying to think of what the hell to do about this terrible situation, but I couldn't think of nothing except only killing ole Peester. The only thing was that just might have some unfortunate consequences on account of I weren't the only peace officer in the area. Ole Dick Custer over at the county seat just might decide to get hisself involved if I was to do something that extreme. I was trying to think of a way I could do the deed and not get him involved in it, but I didn't come up with nothing.

By and by, ole Bonnie come back over, and then so

did Happy, and Aubrey ambled his ass back over to the bar and behind it and went to wiping it off with a rag. I tell you what, I was feeling so hot that if ole Peester had come a walking in to the Hooch House at that very minute, in spite of all my thinking, I would've jumped up and shot him dead. I believe I would have. I'd have did it before I give myself time to think it over. I was that pissed off. Why, I even went and pulled out my trusty Merwin and Hulbert Company .45-caliber self-extracting revolver and kind a fondled it just a little bit.

"Barjack," said Bonnie.

"Whut?" I said.

"Put that goddamned thing away before you do something stupid with it."

"Like blast Peester's ass?" I said. "Hell. He ain't even around."

"Put it away," she said, and she had such a hard look on her face that I done what she said. The next I knowed someone shoved open the front doors and come in, but it weren't Peester nor none of them damn town council bastards at all. No. It was the Widowmaker hisself, ole Herman Sly. He stepped in, and he come walking straight over to us there at my table.

"Drink, Mr. Sly?" Aubrey asked him.

"Coffee," said Sly. He come on over, and I motioned him to a chair. He pulled it out and set down, and he was right across from me. Aubrey brung him his coffee. Sly thanked him and tuck a sip.

"Barjack," he said, "do you know what's going on right now over at Peester's office?"

"Yeah," I said. "I seed them go in there."

"They're having a meeting of the town council," Bonnie said.

"They don't hardly never meet," said Happy. "I figure it must be some kind of emergency or something."

"I'd say that Barjack is the emergency," Sly said.

"I reckon you're right about that," I said.

"Barjack was thinking about killing that Peester," Bonnie said.

"Oh, I wouldn't do that," said Sly. "At least, not yet. And if it does come to that, you need to make him go for his gun first."

"Hell," I said, "he don't even carry none, the cowardly, sniveling, pettifogging son of a bitch."

"Barjack?" said Bonnie.

"Whut?"

"What's pettifogging mean?"

"Never mind," I told her.

"It means a crooked lawyer," said Happy.

"Oh."

"What I would suggest," said Sly, "is that you just sit tight. Wait for them to make the first move. See just exactly what it is they're up to. Then decide what course of action to take. But make it defensive. That's the way I've kept myself out of trouble all these years."

"Defensive," I said.

"Defensive," said Sly.

"Defensive?" said Happy.

"That means don't do nothing 'til they do something first," I said.

"I know that," said Happy.

"And here it comes," said Sly. He was looking toward the front door, and I turned my head to look over my shoulder, and sure enough, here come that little chickenshit Chester. He was looking just a little bit like he'd rather not be coming in there with me, and then he seed that I had some other folks around me too, including the by God Widowmaker, and I thunk for a minute there that he was going to turn his pinched ass around and go back out, but he never. Instead he come on a walking over to the table, and he was holding his hat in both hands in front of him and kind a twisting it around some.

"You look like you done stole some eggs out a my chicken house, Chester," I said. "What the hell are you doing in here this time a day?"

"We're having a town council meeting," he said.

"In here?" I said.

"Well, no."

"Whut then?" I said.

"They sent me over here to fetch you to the meeting," he said, but he weren't looking at me. He was looking at the floor instead.

"They want me at the meeting?" I said, acting like ole Happy by repeating what he just said even though I heared it plain. That always aggravated me about ole Happy, and just then I wanted to aggravate little chicken-shit Chester.

"Yes, sir," he said. "If you don't mind."

Well, that there last thing he said give me just the opening I wanted, and so I said back to him, "Well, I do mind. I ain't getting up from this here chair."

"But—"

"If the goddamned town council wants to see me then they can just haul their ass on over here on account of this is right where I'm at and right where I'm going to stay. So go on back and tell them that. Get on out a here."

I raised my voice just a little bit on that last, and ole chicken-shit Chester, he turned and hurried his little tight ass back out the front door about as fast as he could go. The rest of us just set quiet for a minute or two after that.

"Was that defensive?" Happy final asked.

"Hell, yes," I said. I don't rightly know if it were or not. What it really was was it was calculated to show them bastards just who it was was still in charge of things around our little town there. Sly just set and sipped his coffee. I was glad that he was hanging around too. I never showed it though. I didn't want nobody knowing that I was any unsure of myself in this shitty situation. I drank some more whiskey, and my glass was getting some low. I went ahead and turned it up and drank it down and then held it up high for Aubrey to see, and he brung the bottle. Then they come.

The whole damn town council come walking in, Peester walking in front. He walked them right straight up to my table, and he stood there quiet and looking serious for a minute. The other chicken shits was just waiting on him to make a move. At last he final spoke up.

"Barjack?" he said.

His voice was kind a trembling. I didn't say nothing. I just turned my head a little and give him a look.

"Barjack, we're having a town council meeting."

"Oh," I said. "Is that right?"

"Yes. It is. And we've come to a decision. We—"

"You all have really come to some kind of a decision?" I said. "Now that's remarkable. I never knowed you all to come to no decisions. I might even say that I'm kind a proud of you for that. Made a damn decision. How about that?"

"Barjack," said Peester, "I wish you'd let me talk."

"I ain't stopping you from talking, am I? Just go

right on ahead and talk. I'm listening. Hell, we're all listening here. Go on now."

"We decided—"

"What is it you fellows have gone and decided on?" I said.

"We have decided that it is time for you to retire," he said, and he was a looking as brave and bold as he could manage.

I waited just a little bit to make a response to that startling announcement, and then I said, "Is that it?"

"Well, yes," Peester said. "That's it. That's the decision of the town council. And it's final."

"Well, now," I said, "if the town council makes a decision it sure as hell sure ought to be final. Don't you folks all agree to that?"

"Well, sure," said Bonnie.

"I reckon so," Happy said.

"Town council decisions should be final," ole Sly agreed, and he tuck another sip of his coffee. I tuck a slug a my whiskey and then set the glass back down.

"Well?" said Peester.

"Well, whut?" I said.

"Well, what are you going to do about it?"

"Me?" I said. "Well, hell, I don't reckon I'm fixing to do a damn thing. You made the goddamn decision. I never made it. So I ain't fixing to do nothing about it. Now, you got anymore business with me?"

"We've informed you of our decision," Peester said.

"You've damn sure did that," I said. "So now that you've did it, does the town council have any more further business to deal with?"

"Well, I—"

"Then I suggest that you—what do you call

it?—declare the meeting adjourned. That's the right legal jargon, ain't it? Hell, I'll do it for you." I pulled out my Merwin and Hulbert, and I rapped the butt of it on the table. "I declare this here meeting a the Asininity town council officially by God adjourned. Now you gents can either set down and order yourselfs some drinks, or else you can get the hell out of here and go on about your goddamn business. Whatever the hell you decide."

Peester was looking at that Merwin and Hulbert in my right hand, and he blubbered and blustered a bit, but I never could understand a word he said. Then final he turned around and headed for the door, and the little chicken shits follered him out a there, like baby ducks follering their mama duck.

"Well," said Sly, "you won that round."

"I reckon," I said.

"Oh, Barjack," said Bonnie, twittering around in her chair, and rubbing her big tits against me, "you were just great, the way you told them off."

"Yeah," said Happy, "I reckon you told them off real good."

Sly picked up his cup and finished off his coffee. Then he shoved his chair back and stood up. "I'd best be getting along," he said. "Just remember what I said. That was only the first round."

He headed for the door, and Happy said, "You mean they ain't going to give up?"

"They've gone this far," Sly said. "They can't stop now."

He touched the brim of his hat and walked on over to the door, and then he stopped. He was standing right where the rest of us was earlier and looking out onto the street.

"What is it?" I asked him, and I got up to go over

there and join him. He was looking at Peester and them others, and they was standing on the sidewalk across the street and talking. We couldn't hear nothing they was saying from that distance, and they was talking in low tones anyhow.

"What the hell are them chicken shits up to now?" I said.

Just then they all started walking back toward Peester's office in a bunch.

"It looks to me," Sly said, "like they do not accept your adjournment of the meeting."

As soon as the council got on down the street close to Peester's office, Sly give me a final nod and walked on out. He headed for ole Lillian's fancy eating place. I stood there for a minute and watched him go, and then I turned around and headed back to my place. I set my ass down and picked up my tumbler and had me another drink a good brown whiskey. Everyone was quiet.

"Second round's a coming up," I said.

"They're going on ahead with it?" Happy asked.

"It looks thataway," I said.

"Well, what're we going to do?" he said.

"Just the same as before," I said. "Like ole Sly told us. Wait for them to make a move and then make us our own defensive move. The first move is up to them."

"Barjack," Happy said, "you're just like a rock. Real solid, I mean. I don't know as how I could stand up to something like this myself. I just don't know."

"Well, Happy," I said, "if you don't think you're up to it, then there ain't nothing to hold you here. You can just go on ahead and run out on me in my hour a need like you done once before. I won't even hit you next time I see you like I done that last time."

"I never meant I was fixing to run out on you, Barjack," Happy said. "I meant that I couldn't do what you're doing. Not by my own self. I'm standing right behind you on this. I ain't going to run out on you."

"Well, hell, it's your choice," I said, but I was thinking that I sure was glad ole Happy weren't going to run out on me. I was thinking that before this was all over that I just might need all the help I could get.

"Besides," he said, "I never would a run out on you that last time if you hadn't a told me what you told me. If you hadn't a told me to—"

I looked up at him real quick-like with a hard ass look in my eyes, and he shut up. Course, the reason I done that is on account of I was afraid that the dumb little shit was about to spill the beans on me and say something right there in front of ole Bonnie about how it was that I had told him to shoot her dead if she was to come up behind me that time that I was damn sure she intended to kill me. Even though I had me a good enough reason to say what I said to him, I didn't think it would be such a good idea for him to mouth it out loud right in front of her. I ain't at all sure how she would've tuck it, even after all that time had passed, and even if she had been planning on killing me. I guess Happy tuck my meaning all right, cause he did shut his goddamn mouth.

"All I meant was," he said, "that I never meant to say I was running out on you."

"Well, all right, Happy," I said, backing off on my pissed-offedness a little bit, "I do really and truly appreciate you hanging right in there with me against that gang of chicken shits."

"I'll hang in there with you all right," he said.

"And me too," said Bonnie. "You know that I'll always be right beside you, Barjack, no matter what happens."

Goddamn but I was glad I had shut ole Happy's mouth just in the nick of time.

"Let's go upstairs, sweet britches," she said. "You want to?"

And I sure enough couldn't think of no good reason to refuse her sweet suggestion.

Chapter Five

I walked on down to my marshaling office a little later on that same day just to kind a show Peester and his crew of chicken shits that I was still by God the town marshal of Asininity, and I walked on inside, and then I seen ole Lonnie the Geek a setting in the cell right where Happy had put him the night before. To tell you the whole damned truth, I had total forgot about ole Lonnie. I never let on though. I just walked over to my desk and picked up the keys, and then I went on over to the cell door and unlocked it.

"Come on out, Lonnie," I said.

He come out a little bit hesitant.

"Come on," I said. "You feeling all right?"

"Yes, sir," he said. "I'm a little bit hungry is all."

I reckon he'd done forgot about just how it was he come to be in there. I set down at my desk and wrote him a note, and then I handed it to him.

"Take this here over to Maudie's," I said. "She'll fix you up with a meal. Then once you've et it, I suggest you get your ass on home."

"Can I have my gun back?" he asked me.

"Hell, no, Lonnie," I said. "I don't reckon you got no need for no gun."

He held that note out in front of him and tried to read it, but I don't reckon he could, and then he said,

"Thank you, Marshal," and he went ambling on out of there. It was like I said before, ole Lonnie the Geek, he was all right 'til he got drunked up too much. I went and set down behind my desk, and pretty soon here come ole Happy.

"I seen you come in here, Barjack," he said. "Thought I'd come on in and see if you wanted me for anything."

"Hell, set your ass down, Happy," I said.

He set down, but neither one of us said nothing. We didn't really have nothing to say. It had all done been said over at the Hooch House earlier in the day. I fired me up a cee-gar and went to filling the office up with smoke. Then I pulled open a desk drawer and tuck out a bottle and a couple of glasses. I poured me a drink, and then I looked up at Happy.

"You want a drink?" I asked him, all the while a thinking that it was a dumb question, cause most usually Happy always did want one.

"Sure," he said, and I poured it. He got up and come over to the desk to pick up his glass. "Thanks, Barjack," he said, and he went back to set down again. "I seen you let the Geek out of jail," he said.

"I reckon he was sober enough," I said.

"Yeah."

We was really straining for small talk, and just then, the door come a flying open and who the hell should come a hurrying in but ole Harrison Dingle, the one-time schoolteacher what had wrote that first book about me and then had give up his teaching job.

"Barjack," he said.

"Well, Dingle," I said, "what the hell brings you back to town? I figgered you was all settled down in New York City with them book people."

"Our book has been selling really well," he said. "I brought you a check for your share of the royalties."

He walked on over to my desk and handed me a check. Whenever I looked at it, I got me a real surprise. I never figgered no dime novel would pay me so well, and that after it had done paid ole Dingle too.

"Well, I be damned," I said.

"Pretty good, huh?" Dingle said. "Barjack, you're famous. You're more famous than Wild Bill Hickok. Everyone in the whole country knows your name."

"Is that so?" I said. "Well, now, that makes me wonder how that other damn book is a doing."

"You mean the one that little sniveling plagiarizer Batwing wrote?" said Dingle.

"I never knowed his name," I said. "Batshit is it?"

"I don't know anything about it," said Dingle. "I was in New York dealing with my book when he came out here and wrote that one. He had heard about mine and decided that he would capitalize on its success."

"What was that name you called him?" I asked.

"What?" said Dingle. "I don't remember."

"Hell," I said, "if I knowed the word I wouldn't be asking you."

"Oh," he said. "You mean plagiarizer."

"Yeah. That one. What the hell does it mean?"

"It means someone who steals someone else's ideas," Dingle said.

"And he done that to you?" I asked.

"Well, yeah. He got the idea for his book from my book."

"You reckon he owes me some money?" I asked him.

"It's possible," Dingle said. "But listen, Barjack, as soon as I hit town I heard some interesting talk. I heard that the town council is trying to get rid of you. Is that true?"

"I reckon it's true enough," I said, "but just how the damn story has already got all over town, I sure as hell don't know. How the hell did you get here anyhow? When did you come in?"

"Oh," he said, "I rode the train into the county seat, and then I hired a buggy from there."

"You drive a buggy over here?" I asked him.

"Oh, no," he said. "I hired a driver with it."

Well, that sounded like ole Dingle to me. I never thought he could handle a horse whether it had a saddle on it or if it was hitched to a buggy or a wagon. And that was how come he could slip on into town and me not know about it at first. I decided that since he had brung me such a pleasant surprise in the form of that there check the least I could do was to offer him a drink, so I did, and damned if he didn't accept. I reached back in my desk drawer for another glass, and I poured it about halfway full for him. He tuck it from me, and I said, "Pull up a chair," and he done that and set down.

"Why is the town council trying to get rid of you?" he asked me.

"Hell," I said, "I ain't for sure, but ole Sly, the Widowmaker, you know, he said he figgers they just think they've outgrowed me, whatever the hell that means."

Dingle tuck hisself a sip of my fine brown whiskey, and then he rubbed his smooth chin, and he said, "Hmm. They think they've outgrown you. They no longer have a need for a gunfighting marshal. Is that it?"

I shrugged. "Your guess is good as mine," I said. "All they've told me is that they think I need to retire and take life easy. Hey. Maybe that means they think I'm getting too old for this job."

"Maybe," said Dingle, "but I doubt it. I think that maybe they think that an old-fashioned gunfighting marshal is a threat to future development."

"What?" said Happy, who had kept his mouth shut up 'til this time. He looked at me. "What the hell does that mean?"

I shrugged.

"What it means," Dingle said, "is that they want to attract new business and new people to Asininity. They're afraid that as long as they have you, people will think this is still a wild frontier town and will stay away. That's my guess anyway."

I scratched my head and finished off my glass a whiskey. "I reckon that makes some kind a sense," I said. "At least to a passel a chicken shits."

"So what will you do?" said Dingle. "Where will you go?"

"I ain't going nowhere," I said, "and I ain't giving up my marshaling job neither, and that's my final word on the matter."

Ole Dingle's face lit up like a Roman candle. "Great!" he shouted. "That's wonderful! It's you against the town fathers. The gunfighter standing up to the relentless march of progress. It's another book, Barjack. *Barjack Stands His Ground*, maybe, or maybe, *The Gunfighter Holds His Own*. Something like that. It'll come to me. I'll beat Batwing to the punch on this one for sure. It'll make us rich, Barjack."

"Fuck that Batshit guy," I said. "Hell, Dingle, I can't hardly set around on my ass pondering on getting rich off a no books when I got to be thinking about how I'm going to hang onto my little job here."

"Oh, don't you worry about the book," he said. "I'll take care of that."

Well, I guess I was glad to see ole Dingle back. After all, he had brung me a good chunk a change, and I'll admit that I was kind a puffed up over being made famous and all like that. Dingle wouldn't be no good in a fight, but then this here wasn't shaping up to be no real fight. It would be a different kind a fight, I figgered. And the more I thunk about it, the more I figgered he might do me some good here after all. It was shaping up to be a fight a words, and Dingle, well, he was a man a words. He might just could do me some good in that kind of a fight, and it sure didn't hurt none to have one more on my side.

"Happy," I said, "take ole Dingle here on over to the Hooch House while I go to the bank to deposit this here check. I'll join the both of you over there in just a bit."

So we all left the marshaling office, and I went and done my banking business, and ole Markham, he ducked his head and wouldn't look at me a tall, and then I made my way on over to the Hooch House and found Happy and Dingle and Bonnie all a setting at my favorite table. I went over there and joined them. Bonnie had done ordered drinks all around, so I set down at my place and had me a good slurp out a my glass. Dingle done had his little notepad out on the table and was writing in it with a pencil.

"Let me see that," I said, and I pulled it on over in front a me, and he had wrote at the top a the first page, "Barjack, the famous gunfighting marshal stands up to the town that has decided that it has," and then underneath that he had wrote in great big letters, "NO NEED FOR A GUNFIGHTER." I shoved it back to him and tuck a drink a my whiskey.

"Barjack," said Bonnie, "ain't it nice to have Mr. Dingle back with us?"

"It's nice what he brung me," I said, and I tuck my deposit slip out a my pocket and showed it to her, and her mouth dropped wide open and her eyes got real big. I tucked it back into my pocket.

"What for?" she said.

"It's my share a what he made off a that book about me," I said.

"That's wonderful," she said, looking over at Dingle with some admiring in her little pig eyes.

"It's only fair," he said. He kept on a writing. Then he set back and held up his notebook. "How's this?" he said, and he commenced to reading what he had done writ. "The small town of Asininity was a wild town, one of the toughest in the Wild West, until Barjack came to town. With his two blazing six-guns, he tamed it by bringing to justice the bad Benson outfit. When the last four of the Bensons were released from territorial prison, they returned to Asininity, blood in their eyes, intent on murdering the brave marshal, but he destroyed them all to the last man. Later, he sent the entire notorious Marlin Gang to prison, and then he faced the desperate Jaspers, wiping them off the face of the earth. With the town now a safe place to raise children, the ungrateful town fathers decided that they no longer had need for a gunfighter, and they asked for Barjack's resignation. But they did not count on the marshal's firm resolve. Barjack refused them."

"Oh," said Bonnie, "that sounds elegant. Ain't he great with words? That sounds just elegant, Mr. Dingle."

"Yeah," I said, "the only problem is that we don't know yet just how the hell it's going to end up."

"I have complete faith in you, Barjack," said Dingle.

"Me too," said Happy.

Bonnie give me a hug and a wiggle. "I do too," she said. "My Barjack can handle anything what comes up. I know he can."

I was wishing I had as much faith in my abilities as what the rest of them had. I was wishing that all I had to do was to just face another gang of goddamned owl hoots again and have another fucking gun fight. I was imagining seeing ole pettifogging Peester and them other chicken shits a walking down the street with six-guns strapped on around their waists, and me and Happy and the Widowmaker a walking toward them. But I knowed that would never happen. I tuck me another drink. Then ole Simp come a walking in, and he come right straight to me, and he handed me a piece a paper.

"What's this?" I said.

"You got to sign for it," Simp said.

I jerked the paper out a his hand, and then I jerked the other one, the message I guessed it was.

"You can't do that, Marshal," he said. "You're supposed to sign to prove that I give it to you. That's what I was paid for."

"I don't give a shit about that," I said, and I tore open the message part and read it. I looked up at Simp. "Who give you this?" I asked him.

"Well," he said, "it was the mayor, Mr. Peester."

"You mean it was that goddamned ole pettifogging bastard what has a law office down the street there?" I asked him.

"Well, uh, yeah," he said. "I reckon that is who I mean."

"That cold-blooded son of a bitch what cheats

poor old widow women out a their hard-earned cash?"

"Yes sir," he said. "It was him all right."

"And you're supposed to go back to him with that there paper signed to prove that I got this one here from you and read it? Is that it?"

"Yes sir."

I picked back up the first piece of paper, and I wrote on it, "Fuck you," and I give it back to Simp, and he read what I writ on it, and his face turned kind a white.

"All right," I said. "Take it on back to him."

"Yes sir," he said, and he turned around and hurried on out a there. I picked up the message part again, and I looked around the table at my friends there.

"Well," said Bonnie, "what the hell is it?"

"It says that the town council has met again," I told them. "It says that since I had done refused their first resolution what recommended that I resign, they've done passed a second resolution."

"What is it?" Bonnie said. She never had been much of a one on patience.

"It says they voted unanimous to fire my ass."

"What?" said Bonnie.

"They can't do that," said Happy. "Can they?"

Dingle was writing as fast as he could write. I handed him the note. "Here," I said. "You can have this."

"Thank you," he said, and he commenced to reading it over real careful.

"I reckon they can," I said, and I patted Bonnie's fat little hand what was on the table, "so now it's time for us to play our ace in the hole."

She looked up at me, and I could see that she knowed what I was talking about.

"Play it," she said, "or do you want me to do it?"

"Hell," I said, "I'm afraid that if you was to do it, you'd punch ole Peester's lights out, not that he don't deserve it."

"I would too," she said. "I'd kick his sorry ass down the street in broad daylight."

"No," I said, "I'll take care of that little chore my own self."

"The ass-kicking?" said Happy.

"No," I said. "Playing the ace."

"What is it you're talking about, Barjack?" said Dingle.

"I'm just going to threaten our goddamned honor the mayor," I said, and I stood up. I lifted my glass up and emptied it, and then I said to Bonnie, "You go right on and tell him all about it, sweetie pants. After all, he's a writing a book about me," and I turned around and walked out a there.

Chapter Six

Peester like to've jumped out a his skin whenever I bursted into his office. He stood up and held his hands out in front of him like as if he was defending hisself from my attack, what I never even done to him.

"Now, Barjack," he said. "Now—"

"Set back down, Mr. Mayor," I said. "I got to talk to you, and I reckon it's right serious too."

Well, he set back down real slow and cautious-like, but it looked to me like he was just only perched on the front edge a that chair like as if he wanted to be damn sure he could jump up again real quick-like.

"All right, Barjack," he said. "I'm listening."

"You and me is both working for the same little town, Mr. Mayor," I said, getting right straight to the point a the matter. "We should both of us want the same damn things for it. Don't you reckon?"

"Why, yes. I do suppose that's correct," the prissy shit said.

"Now, you fellas on the town council has asked me to resign, and I was kinda snotty to you. That weren't very nice a me. I know that now. I didn't have no business treating you thataway, and I come here to apologize for it."

"Well, I—I must say—I'm surprised, Barjack. But

pleased. I'm very pleased. And, by the way, we never asked you to resign. We suggested retirement. That's a different matter altogether."

He seemed to relax a little at that. He set on back in his chair, and he even went and smiled. It almost made me feel guilty for what it was I was a fixing to do to him, but it never made me feel guilty enough not to do it.

"So, Mr. Mayor," I said, "I'm fixing to do just that. I'm fixing to resign, but there's something else what's got to go along with it on account a my public spiritedness and all that. You see, Your Honorness, I been carrying around some big secrets inside a me, and I never worried none about them, being town marshal and all, but if it comes to me not being town marshal no more, well, I got to get them secrets off a my chest."

"Well, now, Barjack," His Honorness said, "you could tell me those—secrets."

I shuck my head slow-like as if these deep, dark secrets was really a troubling me, and then I said, "No, Peester, I don't think that would take care of it. Not a tall. I just can't believe that would ease my conscience none. I'm just going to have to make them there little private stories knowed far and wide. Since we ain't got no newspaper, I think that I'm going to have to tell ole Dingle to write up a little book, and then go and have it printed over at the county seat. And then I won't sell it. No, sir. I'll give it away. Spread it out all over the damn county. What do you think about that, Peester?"

"I don't—What stories, Barjack?"

"Oh, just little secrets that some folks around here has," I said. "Not too much. One of them I seem to recall had something to do with a fella name of

Singleterry or Singleton or, no, it was Singletree. That's what it was."

"Singletree?" said Peester, and he went kind a white, and he set back up in his chair and leaned forward some once again.

"I reckon he was gone from here before I hit town, but I heared the story all right. Yeah. Singletree it was. And his wife and there was another feller named Jonsey, I think it was, and it all had to do with who was screwing who both for real and in terms of getting ever'one's money away from them too. And the whole story is gonna—"

"Barjack!" Peester snapped out, and he stood up straight at the same time, and he said, "You can't tell that story."

"Now, Mr. Mayor," I said, "I just can't resign without I get these things off a my chest. I just wouldn't feel no good about it."

"All right. All right. All right," he said, damn near screaming it out. "You win, you rat. Just keep your damned job, and let that be the end of it."

"So I reckon there'll have to be another meeting a the town council," I said.

"Yes," he said, "right away."

I stood up then, and I tuck out a cee-gar and struck a match on his desktop and lit that smoke. Then I puffed at it real hard and fast trying to fill up his little office with my smoke, and I give him a real hard look.

"I want to hear the results a that meeting, Peester," I said. "And then I don't want to hear no more about me resigning, or retiring, or getting my ass fired nor nothing else like that. I don't want to hear no more about it a tall. You got that clear in your goddamned pettifogging head?"

"Yes. Yes," he said. "It's clear."

I walked out a there and on back to my office. I didn't have nothing to do in there, but I was just kind a reasserting myself, I guess you could say. So I went in there, and I set behind my desk, and I tuck out the bottle and the glass, and I had myself a drink a good brown whiskey right there all by my own self, and I put my both feet up on top a the desk. I set there all puffed up like that for a while, and then whenever I'd finished my drink, I got up and headed on to the Hooch House.

When I walked in and on over to my table, I found ole Bonnie and ole Happy and even ole Dingle all a setting there and watching me and damn near holding all their breaths. They was all just a waiting for me to find out what the hell had happened down at the shyster's office, but I never said nothing. I just waved at ole Aubrey, and he brung me a drink about as fast as I got my ass set down. I tuck it up and had me a swaller. Final, I reckon, ole Bonnie, she just couldn't stand it no more. I think I done told you that she didn't have no patience, or at least not much, and she rammed her elbow into my side and yelled out, "Barjack!"

"Ouch! Ow!" I said. "What the hell? Are you trying to break my goddamn ribs or whut?"

"What the hell happened?" she screamed at me.

"I never heard no gunshots," Happy said.

Dingle, he was scribbling.

"Aubrey," I said, "whyn't you go to the front door and kind a keep your eyes out on the street?"

Ole Aubrey didn't say nothing. He just walked out from behind the bar and on over to the front door and just stood there a staring out, and Bonnie and Happy just stared at him. Dingle give him a look but then went back to his scribbling. A cowboy a standing at the bar called out for another beer, but I shut him up.

"Don't be in such a goddamn hurry," I said. "He'll be back over there eventual."

Bonnie started to speak up again, saying, "Well, what—"

But I shooshed her up right quick. "Listen," I said.

"Peester just come out of his office," Aubrey said.

Everyone gawked at Aubrey.

"He's heading for the bank," Aubrey said.

I tuck myself a drink.

"Peester and Markham is coming out a the bank," Aubrey said.

Bonnie jumped up and run to the door, jostling ole Aubrey over some so she could look out there alongside of him.

"They're going into the dry goods store," Bonnie and Aubrey said together.

Happy got up and moved his ass on over to the door to join them. "It looks to me like they're getting the whole town council together again for another meeting," Happy said.

"That's right," Bonnie said. "They're all headed for Peester's office right now."

"They're fixing to have a meeting," Happy said.

"Another meeting," said Bonnie.

"Aubrey," I said, "go on back now and fetch that poor, dry cowpoke there another beer. Happy, you go on down to the office and set behind my desk with your big feet propped up on top of it, and just keep your eye on things. And Bonnie, you get your fat ass back over here and set down by me again."

They all done what I said. Bonnie, she kind a snuggled up against me and wiggled around some, and she looked up at me and smiled real sweet, and she said, "Barjack? What's going on? What did you do to Peester?"

"You just set tight for a spell, sweet pants," I said. "We'll know everything here in just little while," and I tuck myself another drink. Dingle picked up his pad and commenced to reading out loud.

"Oh, the ungrateful wretches!" he read. "The town fathers of the very town that the brave marshal had saved from a terrible fate. The businessmen whose very livelihood had been rescued from lawlessness and terror by the fearless Barjack, the greatest gunfighting lawman in the history of the West. Now that their town was safe for women and children and honest hardworking, patriotic, Christian citizens, the spineless creatures held a town meeting and actually terminated the employment of our hero. The cowardly weasels voted unanimously to fire Marshal Barjack!"

"I like that 'ungrateful wretches,'" I said. "'Ungrateful wretches' is good."

"I'm really partial to 'spineless creatures' myself," Bonnie said. "That's just what they are, 'spineless creatures.' Goddamn them all to hell."

"'Cowardly weasels' is good, too," I said.

Dingle just set there a beaming with puffed-up pride, and then he put down his pad and went back to scribbling. I tell you what, I was sure as hell glad that ole Dingle had popped back up in town. There had been a time whenever I had thunk a him as just only a silly little fart with all his scribbling and his watching me all the time and just being general pestiferous, but by God, I was changing my feeling on him considerable and quite a bit.

Sly come in just then, and he come straight on

over to my table, and I gestured him to set down and join us, and he did. Aubrey called out did he want whiskey or coffee, and Sly said, "Coffee, please," and Aubrey brung it on over to him. Sly thanked him real kindly. He sometimes aggravated me, being so all-fired polite like that, making the rest of us look kind a crude-like, but I still couldn't help liking the son of a bitch. Like I done told you, me and him had been through a whole hell of a lot together, and he had did me some damn good favors too. I reckon he just couldn't help hisself the way he acted. It must a had something to do with the way he was brung up. That's all I can think about it.

"What's the latest news?" he asked.

"Dingle," I said, "read ole Sly here what you just writ." And Dingle went and read again that stuff about the spineless creatures and the ungrateful wretches and all. When he had finished, and he was setting there a beaming all over again, I said, "That there is the latest news."

"I didn't think they'd have the nerve to do that," Sly said.

"Well, they damn sure enough did," I said.

"But Barjack went and seen Peester again," said Bonnie, "and then Peester went and called the town council all back together in his office where they're having another meeting right now as we speak."

"Oh?" said Sly.

"He won't tell us what he said to Peester," ole Bonnie went on. "But we didn't hear no gunshots, and then we did see Peester just walking down the street to get his meeting back together, and he never looked like he was hurt none."

"Now, honeypot," I said, "didn't I promise you that I wouldn't hurt the lawyering bastard?"

"Well," she said, "yes, you did."

"And even that I wouldn't call him no bad names?"

"Yes."

"So why in hell would you been a listening for any gunshots? Tell me that. You done hurt my feelings by thinking about me thataway."

"Oh, darling," she said, snuggling on me again, "I didn't mean to hurt your feelings. I was just so worried is all."

Happy come a running back in then, and he run right over to the table and set his ass down. He seen Sly there, and he tipped his hat. I kind a groaned inside a me on account of it looked to me like as if the Widowmaker's high-toned manners was starting to rub off on ole Happy, and I didn't hardly think I could handle that a tall.

"Happy," I said, "I told you to watch the goddamned office, now didn't I?"

"Yes sir, you sure did," he said.

"So why ain't you watching it?"

"I was watching it, Barjack," he said, "and I was looking out the front winder when I seen Markham and them leave ole Peester's office, and then, what do you think?"

"I don't want to play no guessing games, Happy. Just tell me what the hell you come to tell."

Dingle was scribbling like crazy.

"Well," said Happy, "Peester come out a his office, and he come walking straight over to the marshaling office. I didn't want him to see me peeking out the winder, so I hurried back over to set behind your desk, and I propped my feet up on your desk the way you said, so that whenever he come in, I was just a setting there looking real official and unconcerned."

"All right, Happy," I said. "Get on with it."

Just then, Lonnie the Geek come a walking in and staggered over to the bar and ordered hisself up a drink. When ole Aubrey hesitated some, the Geek slapped his money down on the bar, and Aubrey went and poured him one. I hoped that ole Lonnie had a bundle of cash about his person on account a I didn't want to have to mess with him just then.

"Go on, Happy," I said.

"Well, Peester come on in the office, like I said, and he walked right up to the desk, and he kind a nodded at me, and I said, 'What can I do for you, Mr. Mayor?' and he reached inside a his coat and pulled out this here paper." And when he said that, Happy reached inside his vest and pulled out that paper, and then he just held it up for all of us to stare at. I didn't wait for him to say no more. I just reached across the table and jerked it out a his hand, and I looked at it and turned it over a couple a times. Then I give Happy a hard look.

"Did you read this son of a bitch?" I asked him.

"No sir," said Happy, but I never believed the little snot-nosed son of a bitch. I opened up the letter and read it through. It was official on town council paper and everything just like the last one they had give me, and it read that the town council had done passed another resolution, and with that one they had gone and give me a new appointment as town marshal of Asininity, and this here appointment was for as long as I might want the job. I tossed the paper over to Sly. I ain't sure why I give it to him first, but I done it thataway. He picked it up and read it through, and then he read it through again, only this time out loud for everyone there to hear it. Bonnie shrieked and hugged me so hard that I damn near fell over backward in my chair, but I managed to stay upright, and she final turned me loose.

"Sly," I said, "do you reckon this here calls for a drink?"

"I do, Barjack," he said, "and I'll have one with you."

I waved at ole Aubrey and called for drinks all around, even one for the cowboy what was still at the bar, and even one for the Geek, and pretty soon ole Aubrey had them all served.

"You won, Barjack," Bonnie said. "You actual won."

Happy grinned and raised his glass. "You sure did, Marshal," he said.

Dingle had a drink there in front of him, but he was pretty much ignoring it and scribbling like mad. "Can I see that letter, Barjack?" he asked me, and I passed it over to him.

We set there for a spell having ourselves a victory celebration, and I was feeling like a victorious politician, which I reckon I was at that. I had just won me my first real political campaign for sure. I actual bought two more rounds for ever'one in the house, and Sly actual drank his too. I was feeling real good about myself and my victory, but when Sly got up and made his excuse to leave, he kind a motioned for me to foller after him, and I walked over and joined him about halfway to the door, and he leaned over to say real low in my right ear, "Watch your back, Barjack."

Chapter Seven

Well, now, I had been feeling pretty damn good about my encounter with ole Peester 'til what Sly had said to me on his way out a the Hooch House, and then I got to worrying about it. I decided to just keep them worries to my own self though, at least for a while more. I just went back to my table and set back down and continued on a getting drunk with my friends, all excepting ole Sly, a course. He had gone back to Lillian. By and by ole Happy, he passed out, and then so did Dingle. It weren't too long after that that I sort a lost track a things, and I woked up the next morning, way toward noon it was, upstairs in bed with my Bonnie. I didn't have no idea how it was I got up there.

Anyhow, I got up out a that bed real slow-like, and I stood up easy and picked my way slow-like over to the bowl a water on the little table, and then I splashed my face pretty good. I picked up a towel and dried me off. Then I went and pulled my clothes back on and headed downstairs. I was real careful not to disturb ole Bonnie on account a I remembered real well that time I had woked her up too soon, and she had throwed me headlong down the stairs.

I made my way back down to my table all right, and I yelled at ole Aubrey for a cup a coffee and a tumbler a whiskey. When he brung them over to me, the first thing I done was I drunk about half a that glass a booze. It kind a cleared my head up some, and I felt more than just a little bit better for it. Then I went to slurping on that coffee. I just finished up that cup when I heared a commotion outside what I recognized as the stagecoach a coming into town, and then some kid out in the street yelled out, "Stagecoach is coming!"

Well, now, in a little town like Asininity the stagecoach a coming in to town is a major fucking event. Usual, folks ain't got nothing to do but just work and then drink whiskey, so everyone likes to go out on the street and watch the stage roll in and then see who it is gets off it. I admit that I ain't no exception to that rule, so I stood up and headed for the door. After that good slug a whiskey I had and then that cup a coffee, I felt pretty good.

"Watch my whiskey, Aubrey," I hollered, and then I went on out on the sidewalk. I strolled on down the way a bit so I could have a good look at whoever it was might be coming into my town. I call it my town on account a I'm the town marshal and all, and I sort a makes the rules, and if I don't want someone in my town, well, by cripes, he better just move his ass on down the line. Ole Gooseneck Adams, the driver, hauled up in front a the depot and stopped that team and set the brake, and then he commenced to tossing down the bags that was on top, and then he went to crawling down off a that thing, and at the same time, ole Ash Face Morgan, the shotgun rider, he was going down the opposite side.

"Howdy, Gooseneck," I called out. "Any problems on this run?"

"Not a damn thing, Barjack," Gooseneck said.

Just at that time, a feller come off a the stage, and

when he heared my name called out, he give me a look. I didn't like the look he give me neither, and there was something just a little bit familiar in his face too, but I sure couldn't place it none. He was a city feller by his dress, from back east somewheres. In fact, he looked to me to be from New York City, and I ought to know New York City on account I was there for my first growing-up years, as you might recall. Just about then another dude stepped out a the coach, but I recognized that one for certain. It was that Batshit, the other writing fella, the one what Dingle had called a plagionist or something like that. Well, he sidled up to that other feller in the eastern monkey suit, and it was obvious as all hell that they was traveling companions. They picked up their baggage and headed down the street. I follered ole Gooseneck into the office.

"Gooseneck," I said, "who's that eastern dude you brung in to town?"

"There's two of them, Barjack," he said. "One of them's called Batwing."

"I know Batshit," I said, "but who's that tall tough-looking nut with him?"

"Let's see now," he said, kind a rubbing his chin, "I think his name is something like, uh, yeah, it's Doyle, that's it. Doyle. He come out from New York City riding on a train."

"Doyle?" I said.

"Yeah. That's it. Doyle."

And then it come to me how come me to kind a recognize the son of a bitch. It had been a lot of long years since them days, but it was the little son of a bitch I had beat the snot out of when I was a little son of a bitch in New York City. It was him what had caused me to run away from there and head on out

West. I was running on account a his daddy was a big shot in the Five Points Gang, and I figgered what with what I had did to him, my young life weren't going to be worth a shit around there no more. And now here he was in Asininity after all them years. I just couldn't hardly believe it.

And he had looked at me too whenever he heared my name called. So he knowed who I was, and I sure didn't figger that he had forgot about what I had did to him. It come to me pretty damn fast that he had come all the way out here to get me for that long-ago day. Them Five Pointers, they don't never forget. It come to me then that the reason that bastard was in Asininity was that he had saw them books what was wrote about me by Dingle and by Batshit. I ain't never seed Batshit's book, but Dingle damn sure did name our little town, and a course, he used my real name and had made me famous as all hell. Then I reckoned that Batshit had did the same thing, on account a he was in the company a Doyle.

I went back to the Hooch House, but on the way, I went by my office and found Happy a setting there with his feet on the desk, and I told him to come along with me, and he did. We walked down the street together. I had done told myself after I had saw Doyle that I weren't going to go nowhere without I had me some good company. I thunk it was some ironical, if that's the word for it, that ole Sly had only just the night before told me to watch my ass and then here come Doyle. Me and Happy, we got to the Hooch House and went on in and set at my table, and just about then ole Bonnie come a flouncing and bouncing down the stairs. She spotted me and smiled real big and headed right for me.

I had set my ass down before she got to me, but she

leaned over and smothered my head between her big tits and like to hugged me to death. "Set down, Bonnie," I said. She set down and Aubrey brung her a drink. He knowed what she wanted at that time a day. He looked at me and pointed to my glass, which was still half full, and he give me a questioning look. "Go on and bring me a fresh one, Aubrey," I said, but I picked up the old one to make sure he didn't carry it off, and before he come back with my fresh one I had emptied that glass. He brung Happy a drink too.

The front doors come a swinging open, and I seen Batshit and Doyle come a walking in together. They went right straight to the bar and ordered them both something to drink, and Aubrey brung it to them and collected their money for it. They each one picked up their drinks and had a sip and turned around and leaned their elbows on the bar behind them and commenced to staring at me. Well, I couldn't just set there and take that staring at, so I got up and, taking my drink along with me, walked on over to face them.

"Howdy, Batshit," I said. "Are you a making money off a my name?"

Batshit give a shrug. "I suppose I've made a little," he said.

"That's interesting," I said, "on account a ole Dingle—you know Dingle?—ole Dingle, he's made a bunch off a his book. We kind a speculated that you just might be doing as well as he is."

"I guess I'm doing all right," he said.

"Who's your pal?" I said.

"This is an old acquaintance of yours, Barjack," Batshit said.

"Oh, yeah?" I said, playing dumb and looking Doyle right smack in the face.

"Yeah," Batshit said. "Barjack, this is Butcher Doyle from New York City."

"Butcher Doyle," I said, kind a murmuring, you know. "Butcher Doyle. Doyle. I can't really say that I recall no one with that kind a name. It's a Mick name, ain't it?"

"It's Irish," Doyle said, with a scowl on his ugly mug.

"Yeah," I said. "That's what I thunk. Yeah, I'm from New York City too, but I been gone from there for a hundred years or so, and I'm afraid that I don't recall no Doyles. Why, hell, I don't think I ever even knowed no Irishmen. I reckon you can tell by my name that I sure as hell ain't Irish."

"You met me all right," Doyle said.

"Oh?" I said.

"Yeh," he said. I was kind a enjoying hearing that New York way a talking again. It had been a long time. "I remember you for sure. You done to me something I can't never forget."

"Oh?" I said. "Well, you want to remind me of it?" Course, I knowed exact what it was he was talking about, but I was only just kind a playing with him. I ain't sure how come me to be doing him that way. He sure as hell looked like he could still stomp my ass. Maybe I was just trying to find a way to put off what I knowed was a coming sooner or later, and I was doing what I could to make it later.

"It was just before you left town, Barjack," Doyle said. "We was just kids. You kicked me in the balls, and when I went down, you just kept on kicking me, in the ribs and in the head. You kicked me all over. You might've kicked me to death if your own uncle hadn't come along and stopped you. Your own uncle."

"Oh, yeah," I said, like it was starting to come back to me. "I don't hardly remember no fight, but I do recollect, now that you mention, my ole uncle. How is he these days? Have you saw him lately?"

"He had a heart attack and croaked," Doyle said. "I went to his funeral. It was a real nice one too."

"Well," I said, "I'm sorry to hear that bad news. He was a pretty good uncle to me. And to you too from what you just told me."

"He wasn't my uncle," said the New York dummy.

"Anyhow, I reckon I had ought to thank you for attending his funeral for me," I said, "since I couldn't go to it. Hell, I didn't even know about it."

"You ain't got to thank me for going to the damn thing," Doyle said. "My papa made me go."

"Your daddy?" I said. "How is your daddy? Is he still the head man a the Five Pointers?"

"He is," Doyle admitted. "He's getting kind of old though. I ain't sure how much longer he'll be able to take care of things."

I was starting to get tired a this conversation, and so I said final, "What is it that brings you to my town, Doyle? Did you come all the way out here just to see me?"

"I come all the way out here to kill you, Barjack," Doyle said, "but now that I seen you, I've changed my mind about that."

"So you ain't gonna kill me after all?" I said.

"Nope. That wouldn't hardly be worth the trip no more. I decided that you only beat me up, so I'm just going to beat you up, but I'm going to beat you up even worse than you beat me up. I'm going to beat you up so that you won't never get over it as long as you live, and I hope it will be a long time too."

"That's a pretty tall order, my old friend," I said.

"It's been tried before. I guess you read them books about me. Oh, sorry. You can read, can't you?"

"I can read," said Doyle.

"Well, if you read them books, you know about how a whole bunch a bad asses has tried to beat me up and tried to kill me and what all, and that ain't none of them ever got the job did. So just what the hell makes you think you can do what three or four gangs a bad outlaws ain't never been able to get did?"

"I can take you, Barjack," Doyle said. "I'd have took you that last time, but you caught me off guard. That won't happen again."

I thunk about hauling off and kicking his balls again right then, and I would have too, except that I weren't real sure that my leg could still kick that high, so I decided to let it ride for the time being.

"When you planning on doing this to me?" I asked him.

"We don't think we'll tell you that, Barjack," ole Batshit piped up. Hell, I'd forgot all about him.

"Shut up, Batshit," I said.

"Batwing," he said.

"Shut up, Batshit, I weren't talking to you."

"I'll surprise you, Barjack," Doyle said.

Dingle come into the Hooch House just then, and when he seen Batshit, he stopped and looked awful surprised, and then he stalked right over to face the bastard. He just ignored Doyle standing right there beside Batshit.

"Batwing. You low-life plagiarizing hack writer," he said. "You have your nerve coming back to this town."

"Oh," I said, "he brung a bodyguard with him this trip. This here is ole Butcher Doyle what comes to us from the ole Five Points bunch back in New

York City. He come all the way out here just to kill me."

Dingle looked from Batshit to Doyle. Then he looked at me. His mouth was a hanging wide open.

"You mean that he—"

He was a pointing at Batshit.

"—he brought this man here that wants to kill you—brought him out here and showed him where to find you?"

"That's about it, Dingle," I said.

"Well, I, I—"

He turned on Batshit again. "I'll deal with you later," he said, and he hurried on over to my table and set down between Bonnie and Happy and pulled out his notepad and commenced to scribbling on it.

"Well," I said to Doyle, "if that's all you've got to say to me, then I'll just excuse my ass and go on back over to where my friends is waiting for me, and I'll just be a waiting for your surprise."

I turned my back on them two and went back to my table, still carrying my tumbler full a whiskey. I set back down by Bonnie, and she said to me, "What was all that about?"

"Aw, not much," I said. "You remember that little Batshit writing fella there, the plagiamiser. Well, he went out to New York City, and he looked up one a my old acquaintances there what wants to see me dead, or at least, he did want to see me dead. Now he says he just wants to stomp me up real bad and let me live a long life with some real serious hurts. That's him right there beside Batshit. His name's Doyle."

Bonnie just about come up out a her chair, but I grabbed on to her and held her back.

"Whoa, there," I said. "Just where do you think you're a going?"

"I'm fixing to throw their ass out of this place," she said. "No one can come in here intending to do you hurt and drink our whiskey while he's thinking on it."

"Let them alone, sweet little fat toes," I said. "They got the money, and they're paying for them drinks. We might as well get us as much a their money as we can before this here thing comes to a head."

"Barjack?" said Happy, leaning over toward me. "Is them two some danger to you?"

"They wants to be," I said.

"What do you want me to do?" he asked.

"Just stick close to me is all, Happy," I told him. "Just stick close."

Chapter Eight

Just as them two sissy dressing dudes walked out the front door, ole Dingle looked up from what he was a scribbling, and he yelled, "Hey," and he jumped out a his chair and went running to the door and crashed his way through, and then I heared a damned commotion outside that just compelled me to get up and walk over there and look. Bonnie follered me too. And there was Dingle out there on top of ole Batshit out in the middle a the street just a swinging his little white fists one after the other, some of them a hitting on Batshit and some of them missing. Most of them was missing, I'd say. So I just walked on out there trying to figger out my approach to this interesting situation. Bonnie went to yelling encouragement to Dingle.

I was thinking my own self that there weren't really nothing wrong with a good, healthy fistfight just as long as it was betwixt two growed men what both of them agreed to it. Course, I never knowed what ole Batshit thunk about it, but I knowed that Dingle full approved of what he was a doing. Bonnie damn well approved of it too.

"Get off me. Ow," poor ole Batshit was a howling.

"Stomp his sissy ass," Bonnie yelled.

"Plagiarist," Dingle snarled as he kept on a pummeling with his fists.

"Ouch. Ow. Quit it," cried Batshit. "Ow. You hurt me that time. Ow."

"I mean to hurt you," said Dingle, still swinging. "I'll hurt you all right."

"Smash his nose," Bonnie shouted.

Just then that goddamned Doyle reached inside a his coat and was just about to come out with a handful a British bulldog revolver. Well, by God, I was faster out with my Merwin and Hulbert Company shooter, and I had that son of a bitch aimed right at ole Doyle's balls on account a I knowed that shooter shot some high, and I figgered that if I was to aim at his balls, I just might hit him in the sternum or somewhere around there, and I yelled, "Hold it there."

Bonnie screamed, and Doyle looked at me, and he seed that I had him covered good. He had pulled his little bulldog clean out a the holster, but he hadn't yet turned his hand out to point it nowhere. He stopped still. He just stood there stuck in that there position.

"Drop that little son of a bitch," I said.

He hesitated just a little bit, and then he dropped it, and then I went and cussed myself real good on account I realized the wonderful opportunity what I had just let slip by me. I could a shot the son of a bitch right then. I should have. What the hell was wrong with me? I just weren't thinking, that's all. That's the whole entire truth a the matter. Goddamn it to hell, I thunk to myself. Goddamn it.

So I just walked over toward ole Doyle and kind a backed him up a little bit, and then I stooped over and picked up his little bulldog. I started to tuck it into my waistband, but I couldn't get it in there underneath my belly, and so I final dropped it in my coat pocket. That's what that little thing sold for anyhow was a pocket pistol. Dingle had stopped whopping on Batshit whenever the little whing-ding between me and Doyle had started up, and he was just a setting there on top a Batshit, and the both of them was looking at me and Doyle.

"Butcher, ole buddy," I said, "I reckon you ain't been in town long enough for anyone to a tole you yet that there's a law in this here town against toting firearms in the town limits. So I won't throw your ass in jail on account a you just didn't know, but I'll just have to confiscate this little peashooter a yours."

"That ain't fair," Doyle said. "You're packing one."

"I'm the town marshal," I said.

"I seen other men around carrying guns," he protested.

"Hm," I said. "I never seed them. I'll have to keep me a better lookout, I reckon. Now, I want to tell you something, New York. These two here was having them a bit of a brawl here, and in this here town, there ain't a damn thing wrong with that. Hell, we figger that a good fight can solve more problems betwixt two men than any amount a lawyering. You tried to butt in on that, which is bad enough, but you was fixing to butt in with a goddamn gun. I could throw your ass in jail for that too, but I ain't going to. Not yet. Next time you break a law in this town, though, I will."

I looked down at Dingle, who was still a setting on Batshit.

"Get off a him, Dingle," I said, "and let's go on back in the Hooch House and have a drink. Come on, Bonnie."

Dingle stood up and give Batshit a hard look. Then he dusted off his britches and follered me and Bonnie back on into the Hooch House. We walked straight back to my table and set down, and Aubrey was already bringing us our drinks.

"I'd have thrashed him good," Dingle said, "if that Doyle hadn't interfered."

"It looked like to me you was a getting the best of him," I said.

"You was stomping his ass real good," said Bonnie.

"I should have finished him off," Dingle said.

He was still hot and raring to go. I could tell that, and I knowed just how he felt. There ain't much that's worse in this world than to have someone stop a fight that you have just commenced and you got a righteous feeling about it and on top a that, you're a winning. I had to interfere though when ole Doyle pulled that there bulldog out. I didn't really have no choice. That thought made me think again about what I had did and what I should a did. I was just about as pissed off and frustrated as ole Dingle was. I was still finding it hard to believe that I had not shot the shithead. He'd a been kilt in the line a my duty, and that would a been that. Goddamn it.

Well, now, I got all wrapped up in telling about that little fight and little episode betwixt me and Doyle, and I just went and forgot all about ole Happy, now didn't I? Well, whenever I follered the racket out into the street to see what was going on, and Bonnie follered me, ole Happy had follered the two of us out there too, but he had just kept hisself quiet and just watched what was going on was all he done, so I never really had no reason to mention him no more, now did I? Then I had told Dingle to foller me and Bonnie back in, and he had did that, but ole Happy, he just stood there a staring after Doyle and Batshit.

'Bout the time me and Dingle and Bonnie got our

asses set down and each one of us had tuck a drink out a what Aubrey brung us, ole Happy come back in. He weren't running, but he was walking in a awful much of a hurry. He strid right on over to the table and pulled out a chair and set down and looked right at me, and I knowed he had something what he thunk was important to tell me about. I looked at him back.

"Barjack," he said. "Do you know where them two Yankees went?"

"No," I said, "but I bet you're a fixing to tell me."

"You're right about that," he said. "I'm a fixing to tell you all right."

"Well," I said, "I'm a listening."

"Oh, yeah," he said. "Well, whenever you and Dingle come back in here, them two went walking down the street in the direction a the hotel, but ole Peester, he had been out on the sidewalk a watching, and when they come close to where he was standing, he called them over, and then he invited them into his office, and then they follered him in there."

I didn't want to let on to Happy that he had did real good, but he had. That was news. I recalled what ole Sly had said to me about watching my back, and I knowed that he meant that ole Peester might just be a fixing to try something bad on me, something what might could be permanent. Well, now, here was his first chance. He had saw me take a gun away from that city feller. He hadn't no idea who that feller was, but he had saw what had went on out there in the street. And then he had called to him, and just at that very time, they was in the office a making a deal of some kind. I wondered what it was going to be worth to ole Peester to have me got out of the way—permanent.

"So Peester's a conferencing with Doyle and Batshit," I said.

"Yes sir," said Happy.

"Watch them real close, Happy," I said.

"You done tuck that Doyle's gun away from him," Happy said, "and I don't think that little Batshit even carries one."

"I'll bet you what, ole son," I said. "Before this here day's up, each one of them bastards will be carrying at least one shooting iron with him, but they won't be showing, just like Doyle's bulldog weren't showing."

"Do you think—"

"I ain't thinking," I said. "I know they'll be gunning for me."

"Damn," said Happy.

Ole Bonnie's eyes opened up real wide, and her jaw dropped some, and she looked at me right in the eyes, and she said, "Do you mean—"

"I mean just what I said, honeypot. That goddamned Doyle, he come all the way out here from New York just to get me for what I done to him a long time ago. He was kind a divided betwixt would he kill me or just hurt me real bad. Then ole Peester seen what went on betwixt me and him, and they got all their heads together, and I bet you what. I bet you that ole Doyle's got hisself twice as many reasons now to kill me than what he had when he come to town."

"Oh, Barjack," she said. "Oh."

"And you know what's the worst a the whole damn situation?" I asked. I decided to just go on and tell it to them, and let them see how much of a damn fool I'd made a myself. "Do you know that I could a shot the goddamn shitheaded son of a bitch just a while ago? Whenever he was pulling out that little sissy shooter a his, I could a shot him dead and wouldn't nobody ever a questioned it."

"That's right," said Happy. "You damn sure could have."

"You could?" said Bonnie.

"That's right," I said.

"He's right," said Happy.

"Well, goddamn it, Barjack," she said, "why the hell didn't you do it? Huh? Now you got a goddamn killer lurking around town, and you know he's after your ass, when you could a shot him dead and had it over with and no problems about it. Was that stupid, or what?"

"It damn sure was stupid," I said.

Happy kind a shuck his head real slow like and said, "Barjack, you sure as hell should've shot him dead right then."

"Well, I never done it, now, and I don't want no more said about it," I told them. "Do you both understand my meaning on that? Is you both of you going to shut up about it now? We all know it, and it don't need to be said no more."

"Yeah," said Happy, a hanging his head. Bonnie never said nothing. She just looked in her glass and studied her drink like she was trying to figger out just what it was was in it.

"Happy," I said, "run on down the street to the hotel and see if them two is actual got a room there."

"You mean them two that come in from New York City?"

"Who the hell else would I mean?"

"Well, there's—"

"Go on, goddamn it," I said.

Happy didn't waste no more time. He jumped up

and hurried on out of there, and I reckon that he was headed for the hotel to find out what I told him to find out. Anyhow, soon as he left the place, I quit worrying about him. I couldn't think a nowhere else them two could be staying nohow. I was just wanting to get rid a Happy for a spell, that's all. I picked up my drink and had me a good swaller. I was contemplating on what a hell of a mess I was in. I always figgered that I could handle ole Peester and all them others, but I just never did think that goddamned Doyle kid would show up like that, and just at that time too.

I was a thinking about the last time I seen that little shit. 'Course, he was bigger than me, even back then, but he sure never looked like much lying there in the sidewalk in all kinds a trash, with his knees drawed up to his chest and his arms a hugging his knees, and blood all over his head and puke out on the sidewalk where he had puked it. It damn near made me laugh out loud just recalling on it like that, and then it come to me that I sure as hell couldn't blame him none for coming out here all that way to get even with me. It come into my head that if anyone had left me in that sorry-ass shape and if I knowed where to find the son of a bitch, I'd damn sure be after him myself.

Happy come back then. I didn't think he'd been gone near long enough, but I never said nothing. He come on back to the table and set down again. He put his elbows on the table and stared at me like he was a waiting on me to do something. Final I said, "Whut?"

"I found out," he said.

"What'd you find out?" I said.

"I found out what you told me to find out," he said.

"What the hell are you doing, Happy?" I said. "Are you trying to make me ask you right out in detail what the hell you went and found out about? All right then. Did you go to the hotel?"

"Yes," he said, "I did."

"And did you ask down there was Doyle and Batshit registered there?"

"Yessir," he said. "I asked that."

"And what did they tell you?"

"They told me that Doyle was registered there all right," Happy said, "but they went and told me then that that they didn't have no one named Batshit."

"If Doyle's staying at the hotel and Batshit ain't," Bonnie said, "I wonder where the hell Batshit is a staying." She wrinkled her face and scratched her head.

"That's kind a what I was thinking back at the hotel," Happy said, "but then the clerk said to me, 'We got a man named Batwing here,' and I knowed then that was his real name. It ain't Batshit, Barjack. It's Batwing. I bet you didn't know that."

I was thinking that ole Happy could easy a come into the place and set down and said, "Yeah. They got rooms there," and that would a been it. That would a tole me all that I wanted to know. But Happy had got something up his ass, and he had to go through all that bullshit before he could tell me that simple little goddamn thing. I thought about throwing him outside in the dirt or busting him in the jaw or something, but then I decided that it just wouldn't be worth the trouble.

"Just pick up your drink and drink from it," I said.

He did, to my everlasting relief. And Bonnie had gone quiet too. Of a sudden, I was setting there in the midst a Bonnie and Dingle, who was scribbling again, and Happy, but it was like I was just all by my own self. It was quiet. I needed that quiet too, and I commenced to thinking about things. I thunk about my job and the way I had done saved that. I had me a paper from the pettifogger hisself that said I had my job for as long as ever I wanted it. I had felt good about that too 'til ole Sly had told me to watch my ass, meaning, I figgered, that Peester just might hire someone to blow my ass away. I was just beginning to come to grips with that sort a unsettling thought, when that damned Doyle come to town. I never put the two together. I just knowed that Doyle had come after me, and then Doyle and Peester had got their heads together, so both a my enemies was now ganged up on me, and I didn't know what the hell to do about it. It come to me that I needed some serious counseling, and the only serious enough counselor I could come up with in my head in that there little town a mine was that gunslinging widowmaking son of a bitch, Herman Sly.

Chapter Nine

It were the next morning before I seen ole Sly, on account a I didn't want to go over to his house where he lived with his wife and my ex-wife, ole Lillian, what had tried to shoot me to death one time and had actual nicked off a piece a my ear in the trying. So I waited 'til they was walking downtown a heading for her place a business. As they walked down the street, I kind a give a nod, and Lillian, she nodded back and stuck her nose in the air, but ole Sly, he waved and give me a look, and I kind a give a jerk with my head to let him know I wanted to visit some with him. He nodded back at me, and whenever he had got ole Lillian walked to her fancy eating place, he must a made some excuse and headed on over to the Hooch House. Bonnie was still upstairs asleep, and ole Happy hadn't showed hisself yet that morning. I don't know where the hell Dingle was at. Sly come in and found me setting at my table, and I yelled at Aubrey to bring over two cups a coffee. He brung them, and Sly come over and set down. "Morning, Barjack," he said.

"Morning, Sly," I said.

We both of us sipped from our hot coffee, and then Sly said, "Was there something you wanted to see me about?"

"I don't know if you heared anything," I said,

"but yesterday that ole boy from New York City, the one what come all the way out here just to get me, he went and had hisself a talk with ole Peester. Him and that Batshit writing feller. Course I can only just guess at what they was a talking about, but then, I reckon my guess would be pretty damn good."

"I suspect you'd be right," Sly said. "Who initiated the conversation?"

"Who whut?" I said.

"Did Doyle just go see Peester on his own or—"

"Oh," I said. "I get you. No. Ole Peester was a watching whenever I had a little set-to with Doyle out in the street, and then when Doyle and Batshit was a walking by, why, the ole pettifogging bastard called him on over to his office."

"So what do you make of it, Barjack?" he asked me.

"Well, you know," I said, "ole Peester, he give me that new contract, if that's what it is. He give me that letter what says that the town council a this here town has give me back my job for just as long as I want it."

"Yes," he said. "I know that."

"Well, only, you know," I said, "he never really wanted to do that a tall. He wanted to fire my ass like he done 'til I called him on it. You see, I know a little secret on that son of a bitch, and I kind a let it slip out that I might just let that old story get out in public, you know? That's when he had that second letter drawed up and give to me."

"So you had him over a barrel, so to speak?" said Sly.

"Yeah. I reckon that's one way a putting it all right. Well, then, I reckon he was a feeling whipped 'til he seen me have that set-to with ole Doyle, and then I figger that he seed Doyle as a possible way out a his dilemma."

"He might be able to talk Doyle into doing away with you for him," said Sly.

"He likely offered Doyle some money to do the job," I said. "Hell, he wouldn't even a had to talk him into nothing. That's what Doyle come out here for in the first damn place."

"That was good luck for Peester all right," Sly said. "Do you want my advice on the matter? Is that why you called me over here?"

"I sure wouldn't mind it none," I said. I turned up my cup and drank down all a my coffee. Sly finished his off too. Ole Aubrey seen us and come over with the coffeepot. Sly let him pour some into his cup, but I said no. I told him to bring me a tumbler a whiskey, and he went off to do that. Sly set there a bit looking all fired thoughtful.

"Barjack," he said, "the only thing I know to tell you is to watch Doyle real carefully. Don't ever turn your back on him or on that other one. What's his name?"

"Batshit is his name," I said. Sly give me a curious look.

"Batshit?" he said. "Well, all right. Keep your eyes on both of them. Keep Happy close by, and I'll stick close as much as I can. The best we can do, I think, is to try to catch them trying to get you in their sights. Anything else would be murder."

Aubrey brung me my whiskey, and I tuck me a slug of it. "I kind a figgered you'd say something like that," I told Sly. He give a shrug.

"You can't just gun a man down because you think that he's planning to gun you," he said. "The law looks dimly on that."

"I could kick myself in my own ass," I said.

"What for?" Sly asked me.

"I had my chance yesterday," I said. "Ole Doyle, he was pulling a gun out to use on Dingle, and I pulled mine first and told him to hold it. I should a just shot him dead right then and there."

"That was a chance all right," Sly said.

"Well, I blew it all right." I said. "Goddamn me." I tuck me another drink then, and Sly waved at Aubrey. Aubrey come over to the table, and Sly ordered hisself up a breakfast a ham and eggs. Aubrey went to get it started, and Sly said to me,"I'm going over to tell Lillian what I'm up to. Then I'll come back over here and hang around." I said okay, and he went on out. I tuck another drink. Sly was gone a little bit longer than I figgered he'd ought to be, and he just barely got his ass back in time for his breakfast. He set back down, and Aubrey set his breakfast down in front of him.

"Thank you, Aubrey," Sly said. "Barjack, guess who's over at the White Owl having breakfast?"

"Not ole Happy?" I said.

"Not hardly."

"You mean them two? Doyle and Batshit?"

"That's right," he said.

"Well," I said, "at least they ain't at my back."

Happy come in at last, and he come over to my table and ordered hisself a breakfast from ole Aubrey. He said his good mornings to me and to ole Sly, and then he said to me,"Where do you want me this morning, Barjack? Over to the office or just right here?"

"You stick your ass to me today, Happy," I said. "Wherever I go, you go."

"All day long?" he asked me.

I heaved a sigh. "Happy," I said, "what the hell did I just now tell you?"

"To stick to you today," he said.

"So you just do that, will you?" I said. "Don't ask me if I want you on my right side or on my left side or walking back behind me. Don't ask me no goddamn questions. Just do what the hell I told you to do."

"Okay, Barjack," he said. It never even bothered him getting fussed at thataway. I often wondered if he even knowed he was being fussed at or made fun of or anything like that. Hell, he might a actual enjoyed it. Sly finished up his breakfast, and he stood up.

"I'm going back over to the White Owl," he said, "and keep an eye on those two."

"Sure thing," I said.

As Sly walked toward the door, Happy looked at me and said, "What two?"

"Hell," I said. "I don't know."

Aubrey brung him a cup a coffee and set it down and said, "Your breakfast will be ready in just a minute."

"Thanks, Aubrey," Happy said, and it come to me again that ole Sly's politeness was a rubbing off onto Happy. Then the front doors swung open wide, and ole Dingle come in and joined us. When he set down he pulled his damn notepad out a his pocket and laid it on the table in front of him. I was kind a glad he didn't open it on up and start in to writing yet. I knowed he would before too damn much longer. It was on account of his goddamn book that Batshit had writ his book, and it was the fault a both a them books that I was in this trouble with ole Doyle here in town after my ass and in league with Mister Mayor, pettifogging Peester. I couldn't quite put all the blame on ole Dingle though. Like I done told you, I had sort a begun to take a liking to him. Sort a.

Well, Happy got his breakfast, and he tore right into it. I tell you what, none a Sly's manners rubbed off on him when it come to eating. He just wolfed it on down. And Dingle ordered hisself some too. Now, I'd had about enough a all that, so I told Happy, "Get up and come along with me," and then I said to ole Dingle, "We'll be back here in just a little short time." Dingle said okay, and I led Happy out a the Hooch House.

Whenever we got out onto the sidewalk, Happy asked me, "Where we going, Barjack? We going on down to the office are we?"

"Never you mind where we're a going," I said. "Your job is to just stick to me. Remember?"

"Yeah," he said. "I remember all right."

I strolled on down the street 'til I come to Peester's office, and then I just barged right on in, and Happy, he come in right after me. I went on over to the next office and stomped my way on in there, and ole Peester, he was setting behind his desk. He looked up right surprised, and I said, "Good morning, Mister Mayor. How are you doing this fine morning?"

"Why, uh, I'm all right," he said. He was looking at me like as if he wanted to say, What the hell are you doing in here? He never said it though. He just set there. I pulled up a chair and set it right across the desk from him, and then I motioned at another chair.

"Set yourself down, Happy," I said, and he done it. I tuck out a cee-gar and then I struck me a match on the arm a the chair and lit my smoke. I puffed it out as much as I could do right toward ole Peester, and I could see that it bothered him some. I tossed the match down on the floor. "I heared," I said, "that you met my old buddy what is visiting us all the way from New York City."

"What?" he said. "Why I—"

"You did meet him, didn't you?" I asked.

"Well, yes. I guess I did."

"You guess?" I said. "Well, did you or didn't you? If you never met him, like what I heared, I'll have to bring him right on over here and interduce you. He's a old friend of mine from back when I still lived in that damn city. You knowed that I was from New York City, didn't you?"

"No," he said. "You never told me that."

"Well," I said, "I am. I growed up my first few years back there, but I left it when I was still a young shit to come and seek my goddamn fortune in the West. But I knowed him back there. I sure did. Doyle's his name. They call him Butcher. Ole Butcher Doyle. It was damn sure a real surprise to me whenever he come in to town. I never expected no visits from back there and that long ago. No sir. I never."

"Well, uh, yes," said Peester. "I did meet Mr. Doyle. Mr. Batwing, the writer, brought him in to meet me. I guess that Mr. Batwing just thought that a visitor from New York should meet the mayor. So I met him. That's all. I didn't know he was an old friend of yours."

Well, a course, I knowed that Peester was lying to me on account a I knowed that it was him what had waved at Doyle and Batshit to come on over to see him, and then he had tuck them both into his office for a private talk. I knowed all that, but I never said nothing about it. I was just there to kind a tease ole Peester and maybe to make him wonder if his little deal with Doyle was a working out or not.

"I'm just tickled that you met with him, Peester," I said. "Whenever a man comes all that goddamn distance for a visit, he had ought to be greeted real proper by the mayor. What did you think about Mr. Doyle, Mr. Mayor?"

"What did I think of him?"

Now Peester was talking like Happy, always asking for thing to be said again. "That's just what I asked you," I said.

"Why, I don't know," he said. "I suppose I found him personable enough."

I wondered just what he meant by that word "personable," but I never asked. I just pretended like as if I knowed. "Peester," I said, "has you ever heared about the Five Points Gang?"

"The Five Points Gang?" he said. There he done it again. "Why, no. I don't believe I have. Is that a new outfit operating around these parts?"

"It's a real old outfit," I said, "and it operates in New York City, and Mr. Doyle's daddy, he's the big boss a that bunch. Mr. personable Doyle is a Five Pointer. He has been all his life. He's a big-time gangster. Him and all them Five Pointers. They operate a protection racket, and they robs things, and they kills people. That's their business. It's big business too. In New York City nobody fucks with the Five Pointers. No sir. If they do, they wind up deader'n a goddamned dinosaur."

Peester went to stammering the way he always does whenever he gets nervous, and I stood up and headed for the door. Standing in the doorway, I turned on back around, and I said, "I just thunk that you might ought to know about that." Then I said, "Come on, Happy," and Happy stood up and follered me back out a Peester's office. Out on the sidewalk I stopped and just stood there for a minute, hooking my thumbs in the armpit holes a my vest and smiling.

"That felt real good, Happy," I said.

"Was it true?" he said.

"Was what true?" I said.

"All them things you said about Doyle and the Five Points Gang and all that," he said. "Was they true?"

"They damn sure was, Happy," I said. "Ever' goddamn word. They're going to keep after me now that they found me for as long as I live."

"Well, Barjack," he said, "what're we going to do about it?"

"We ain't going to do nothing 'til they makes a move," I said. "That way, whenever we kill one of them, it'll just be self-defense is all."

"You mean that if we was to kill this here Doyle," Happy said, "that there Five Points Gang'll just send another one out here to get you?"

"That's about the size of it," I said.

Just then Doyle and Batshit come out a the White Owl and turned toward the hotel, which meant that if me and Happy stayed right there where we was at, they would have to walk right past us. They come a little ways in our direction, and then I seed Sly come out and stop just outside the fancy eating place and watch them. He seed me and Happy too, so he was watching real careful-like. He went and follered them a few steps too, I figgered so that his shot wouldn't be too long a one if he was to have to make a shot.

"Don't step aside, Happy," I said, and me and him just kept our place there on the sidewalk so that Doyle and Batshit would have to step down into the street to get past us. They kept a coming on, and by and by they was just about up to where we was at, and then when they come up to us, why, they stopped. "Howdy, boys," I said. "How's our little town a treating you?"

"All right, I guess," said Doyle.

"You all have a good breakfast?" I asked them.

"It was good enough, I guess," said Batshit.

"If I was you," I said, "I wouldn't say nothing too bad about the grub you get in the White Owl Supper Club or whatever it is they're a calling it now. See that feller watching you from down the street?"

I gestured toward ole Sly, and they went and turned around and looked back at him. His coattails was throwed back to show off his two six-guns and to make it easier for him to grab at them.

"That there," I said, "is ole Herman Sly. He's a professional killer, a gunfighting man. And it's his wife what owns and runs the White Owl. If you was to say anything bad about the place, why, he just might shoot you down without no warning. He's awful protective over his wife."

"We had a good breakfast," Doyle said.

Chapter Ten

Well, now I figgered I had ole Peester buffaloed all right on the legal end of things, at least what with that new contract letter I had got out a him and all, but then there was the other possibility, and what that was I was thinking was that ole Peester just might be planning on having someone shoot me in the back to solve his problem. He had done had hisself a talk with ole Butcher, and I figgered that he was up to something rotten and sneaky-like at that time. I had to figure out me some way to keep my ass safe from political assassination no matter what it was that was about to come up, and that from now on for the rest of my natural life.

Well, I was out walking on the street headed from my marshaling office back toward the Hooch House, and it was coming on sundown, and I seed ole Butcher just a standing in the street just about in front of the Hooch House, and then I seed that Batshit standing maybe twenty-five or thirty yards away from Butcher and facing him. My path was fixing to lead me right betwixt them. I hesitated just a bit, but I sure as hell didn't want them thinking that they had me skeered or nothing like that. Just then good ole Happy Bonapart stepped out the front door a the Hooch House and just kind a stood there on the sidewalk and looked around. He for sure seed what the situation was like, and I went on and continued my way toward my intended destination.

I never thought that Batshit was nothing to worry about, so I was kind a keeping my lookout on ole Butcher Doyle, kind a out a the corner a my eyes, and just as I stepped right in betwixt them, just about midway betwixt the two of them, and I was a watching ole Butcher, Happy called out, "Barjack, behind you!"

I ducked and hauled out my Merwin and Hulbert and whirled around toward that goddamned little Batshit, but before I could even raise up my gun to point at him, a shot rang out from back behind me, and that snotty Batshit staggered back a step. He was holding a shooter in his hand, but his hand begun to droop, and he staggered some more, and then he fell over onto his face in the dirt. I whirled around to face Doyle again, and I seed him lowering down his shooting hand, and it was holding a smoking six-gun. I looked back at Batshit lying there in the street and not moving a tall, and I looked back at Butcher, who was by this time tucking his gun away back under his coat. Happy come walking down into the street, and went straight over to Batshit and bent over him.

"He's dead," he said, straightening up again. He come walking over to my side. I was still standing there with my gun in my hand looking around me trying to figger out just what the hell was going on and whether or not I had ought to shoot somebody, and Happy said, "Batshit was about to back-shoot you, but Butcher shot him first."

"Butcher done that?" I said.

"Yes sir," said Happy. "He sure as hell did. It was a hell of a good shot too."

Butcher had turned around and was about to walk off, but I yelled him down. "Hey, you, Butcher," I shouted. He stopped and turned back around to face me. I walked on over to him and looked him square in the eyeballs. I jerked my head back toward the stiff a lying in the street. "What the hell was that all about?" I asked him. "I thought you and him was pards."

"I just didn't want him shooting you in the back," he said. "That's all. He told me you was out here, and he brought me here all right, but it was so I could whip your ass or kill you my own self in a fair fight. That's all."

"So you still wanting to whip my ass?"

"It would make me feel better," he said.

"Well, now," I said, "I reckon you know that I could throw your ass in jail for getting yourself ahold of another shooting iron."

"I guess," he said.

"But I s'pose I could overlook that there little transgression being as how you went and saved my ass by killing Batshit."

"You think you could do that?" he said.

"I sort a make the rules around here," I said. I unbuckled my gun belt and handed it to Happy. "Hand your gun over here," I said, and Butcher reached under his coat and pulled it out and give it to Happy. "You just hold on to them for a spell," I said. Then I looked back into Butcher's eyes again, and I said, "Well, by God, let's get it on." He looked at me curious-like, and I said, "You told me twice now that you're a wanting to whip my ass. Well, get it on."

And without no warning he swung his right hand and smacked me a damn good one along the side a my head. It spun me around and staggered me for sure, but I never fell down. I kind a shook my head some to clear it up, and then I put up my dukes and moved in toward him. He was a big one for sure, some bigger than me, but I never let that stop me none. He put up his own dukes and stepped toward me, and I kicked out with my right foot catching him on his left shin. He howled and hopped on his right foot while reaching for his left leg. He danced around like that in circles for a spell, and I let him, but then I decided that I had let it go on long enough, and when he danced around facing me again, I let him have it. I popped him a right cross to the side of his head and sent him sprawling in the street.

Well, now, I could a commenced to kicking him about the head and the ribs and doing his ass in the way I done it before whenever we was just kids in New York City, but something kept me from doing that to him. It might a been on account a he had just killed Batshit for me, or it might a been 'cause we went back so far together, the two of us, or it, well, hell, it might a been on account of I had begun to kind a like the son of a bitch. Whatever it was, I just stood there waiting for him to get up and trying to be as ready as I could ever be for whatever it might could be that he was a fixing to throw at me.

Anyhow, he eventual stood on up on his feet, and he done what I done before. He stood there a shaking his head to clear it on up. He give me one a the meanest looks I had ever been give, and I'd been give a plenty of them in my time. It skeered me just a little bit, and I wondered if maybe he had another gun hid about his person somewheres. But he never went for one. He just come right at me, and whenever I went to kick him in the shins again, he sidestepped it real neat-like. That missed kick throwed me off a my balance, and he tuck advantage a that. He went and jabbed me in the face, right on the end a my nose, and it stung like hell. I remember thinking at the time that he had broke it. While I was trying to recover from that sharp smack, he hit me again on the side a the head, and then he driv a hard right into my gut, which had become some paunchy in recent years. I doubled over at that, and he raised up a knee into my face. Well, that knocked me over, and I sprawled in the dirt.

He never waited for me to get up the way I done for him. He leaned over and grabbed me by my coat lapels and picked me up, and he went to backing me up. I didn't have no control. He shoved me right back 'til I was up against the watering trough there in the street, and he pushed me over and into the goddamn trough. I went clean under the water, splashing it out all over the place, and whenever I come up for air, there was a whole bunch a folks lined up on the sidewalks just a laughing like hell at my dilemma. I went to trying to lift my ass out a there, and I was slipping and sliding and falling back in, and I seen that son of a bitch Five Point bastard Doyle a laughing harder than any a the rest. It like to made my blood boil, but then he stepped over and held out a hand toward me.

I give him a curious look, and he was still a smiling. I tuck his hand, and he helped me out a that trough. I stood there shaking myself like a wet dog, and Butcher said, "Well, Barjack, I guess we're even now after all them years." I damn near said, "No, we ain't even. This here fight ain't over with yet," but I held my tongue. It come to me just then that my troubles with the Five Points Gang was over with. I decided to let him go on believing that he had whipped me. He had the whole damn town laughing at me. He was feeling good about it too. Hell, he had saved my worthless hide from getting blowed all to hell, and then he had went and whipped my ass, so he thought. I let it go at that. I held out my hand to him, and he tuck it, and we shuck hands.

"You whipped me fair and square," I said. "Come on in the Hooch House and let me buy you a goddamn drink."

"All right," he said.

As we stepped in front a Happy, I held out my hand, and Happy give me back my gun belt, and I said to Happy, "Give him back his gun."

Happy give me a curious look, but he done like I told him to do, and Butcher tuck his revolver and tucked it back under his coat. We walked inside and went on over to my private table and set down. Aubrey brung me a tumbler a my private good whiskey, and I said, "Bring him the same." In another couple a minutes me and Butcher and Happy was all a setting there sipping good whiskey, and then I seen Bonnie a coming down the stairs with her ample bosoms just a bouncing. She come over and set down beside me, giving a strange look at ole Butcher a setting there peaceful-like with me at my table.

"Darling sweet hips," I said, "this here is my old pard from New York City, Butcher Doyle. He just went and broke my nose. Happy, straighten it out for me."

I turned my chair sideways so I could lean back and put my head against ole Bonnie's big tits, and then Happy stood up and walked around the table. He stepped up real close, a straddling my legs, and he bent over me and put his hands on my face. I tuck a deep breath preparing for the sharp pain that I knowed was about to follow. Happy had did this before for me more than once. He stuck a thumb up against my sore nose real tight, and it hurt like hell, and then he shoved it to one side right quick, and as the world went black and then red, I heared it snap into place. I yowled out loud, skeering ever'one in the Hooch House, and I lay there against them monstrous tits for another minute or two, and then I final set back up and kind a shuck my head a little bit. Happy had done gone back to his chair and set down.

"Thanks, Happy," I said.

"Shore, Barjack," he said.

Bonnie give me a curious look and said, "He broke it?" She was nodding toward ole Butcher.

"He damn sure did," I said. "He's a hell of a fighter."

"Well," she said, kind a hesitating, "what's he doing here with us?"

"I done told you, didn't I?" I said. "He's my old pard. We was kids together back in New York."

"But—"

"Never mind, sweetness," I said. Then I picked up my glass and tuck me a long slug a that good brown whiskey. I sure did need it after that there ordeal with my nose. I set my glass back down and looked over at Doyle. "There's still that matter a you toting a firearm in my town," I said.

"You want it, Barjack?" he asked me. "I ain't going to tell you where I got it."

"I never thought you would," I said. "I never considered you to be no snitch."

He reached under his coat to get the gun, but I stopped him. "I know a way you could keep on a carrying that gun with you," I said. "That is, unless you're in a big hurry to get your ass back to the big city."

"I ain't in no big hurry to do nothing," he said.

"Well," I said, "since you ain't in no hurry, if you'd like to be able to keep on a toting that there firearm, I could make you a deppity marshal in this here town."

His jaw kind a dropped open and his eyes popped open wide in disbelief.

"Happy," I said, "run over to the office and fetch me back here a badge." Happy stood up about halfway, looking stupid, and I looked over at ole Butcher. "Unless you got some objections," I added.

"It sounds kind a crazy," Butcher said, "you making me into a lawman. Me, of all people. You ain't kidding me, are you?"

"Like I said, you got any objections?"

I picked up my tumbler and tuck me another long drink and held up the empty glass for Aubrey to see. He come hurrying on over with the bottle to fill it up again, and while he was at it, he filled up the other glasses too. Butcher grinned a wide grin.

"I ain't got no objections," he said.

Happy was half standing up, and I give him a look. "Get on now," I said, "and fetch that badge over here." He went hurrying on out a the place, and on the way he damn near run over ole Dingle, who was just coming in. Dingle watched after Happy for just a few seconds, and then he come on over to the table and looked at Doyle with a strange look on his face.

"Set down, Dingle," I said. "You know Mr. Doyle here?"

"I, uh, I don't believe we've met formally," he said.

"Well, shake hands," I said. "Doyle is my old pard and my most recent depitty."

"Deputy?" said Dingle.

"Don't I talk plain enough?" I said.

"Deputy. Yes," said Dingle. He reached out a hand and shuck with ole Butcher.

"Dingle here is a writing all about my exploits out in the Wild West," I told Butcher.

"Yeh," he said. "I know about Dingle's books."

"Well, Scribbler," I said to Dingle, "I don't know where you was at, but you missed a damn good show just a few minutes ago."

"Oh?" he said.

"Butcher here killed that goddamn Batshit out in the street."

"Killed?" said Dingle.

"Saved my ass too," I said. "Batshit was a fixing to gun me in the back."

"Well, I'll be—"

"And then ole Butcher went and broke my nose for me and throwed me in the horse trough."

"Wait a minute," said Dingle, hauling out his notepad and a pencil. "I don't understand any of this. I—"

"Calm down, Scribbler," I said, and I waved at Aubrey and pointed to Dingle, and Aubrey come at us in a minute with a drink for Dingle. He set it on the table in front a Dingle, and I said, "Now drink up and settle down, and we'll tell you all about it."

Well, he did, and betwixt me and Butcher, we told him the whole story, even going on back to when we was kids in New York City and how come Butcher had come to Asininity in the first place. Dingle was writing real fast-like as if his whole life depended on it, and then, here come Happy back from the office. He come back to the table and handed me a badge, which I tossed over to Butcher.

"Pin that on," I said.

Butcher picked it up and looked at it, and he

looked down at his chest, and then he looked back up, and he said, "Where do I pin it?"

"Any goddamn place," I said.

He final pulled his coat off to one side and pinned the badge onto his vest on the left side right where the hell it was s'posed to be in the first place. He leaned back in his chair looking smug as hell.

"You're a depitty now," I said. "It's official."

"Don't I have to swear or something?" he said.

"No, hell," I said. "What we have to do is we have to get good and drunk to celebrate this new arrangement."

I was feeling real good now that I had me two depitties again and that at a time when I might just need them real bad. I tried my best not to show my genuine joy, and I never told none of them about my suspicions about ole Peester maybe hiring some gunfighters to come to town and kill me, but I sure did feel good about having ole Butcher on my side in case a trouble. He was one badass son of a bitch, I mean to tell you. I drank my glass empty again and held it up for Aubrey to see, and he come running to the table with the bottle.

Chapter Eleven

Well, it was around midmorning a the next day when I come awake, and it tuck me a minute or two to figger out that I had been a sleeping it off in a jail cell. I reckoned that ole Happy had tuck care a that. He had did it often enough in the past. I groaned and moaned and final set my ass up on the edge a the cot and held my head in my hands for a spell. Then I went to coughing, and I hacked up a lunger and spit it out on the floor. Then I heared a voice, and I looked up to see ole Happy peeking at me through the bars.

"Barjack?" he said. "Barjack, are you all right?"

"Hell, yes," I said. "I'm all right. Why shouldn't I be? Fetch me a drink a whiskey out a my desk drawer."

"Barjack?" he said.

"What?"

"What about him?"

"Him who?" I said, and I seen Happy nodding his head in the other direction, so I looked up and across the cell, and I seen ole Butcher laid out on the other cot still a sawing logs. "Oh, him," I said. "He's sleeping real good. Just leave him be."

"Okay," Happy said, and he walked over to the desk. In a minute he come back and stepped in the cell to hand me a tumbler full a whiskey. I tuck myself a big swig a that wonderful stuff, and my head cleared up right away. Damn, that's good medicine.

"You s'pose he's all right?" Happy asked me.

"Him?" I said. "Oh, hell, yeah, he'll be just fine. It's just that he ain't in good shape the way I am for drinking. That's all. Give him a little more time with me, and he'll come around. I'll get him in shape all right. You got to remember, Happy, ole Butcher has spent his whole life in that sissy place, New York City. He weren't lucky enough to get out a there at a young age the way I was."

I was thinking even when I said that about what a rough son of a bitch New York City really was, but I weren't about to let ole Happy in on that.

"Yeah, Barjack," Happy said. "You surely was lucky to get out a there whenever you did."

Ole Butcher groaned and rolled over just then, and he went and rolled right off a the cot and landed with a big splat on the cement floor a that cell. He reached up and tuck hold a the edge a the cot and kind a pulled hisself up to a setting position, holding on to his head with his extry hand. He just set there moaning, and I told Happy, "Fetch him a drink too."

Happy was back in just a minute and held a glass out to Butcher, but ole Butcher, he just kind a waved it away.

"Take it, Butcher," I said. "Drink it up. It'll sure as hell make you feel better."

"Hell," he said, "I done had too much last night."

"You ever heared the old expression, hair a the dog what bit you?"

"Huh? Yeah. Sure, I heard it."

"Well, that right there in that glass is what they're talking about whenever they say that expression. It's damn good medicine. Drink it down now."

Butcher tuck the glass from Happy, and he held it in front a his face and stared at it for a spell. Then he sniffed at it and made a face.

"Go on," I said. "Drink it."

Well, he tuck a sip and kind a wrinkled his face up as he swallered it down. Then he tuck another sip, and then he drank down the whole damn glassful. He put the glass down on the floor and pulled hisself on up 'til he could set on the edge a his cot, and he blinked his eyes and rubbed his face with both hands, and I could tell he was already feeling better.

"Happy," I said, "is there any water in that bowl in the back room?"

"Yes sir," he said.

I got my ass on up and said to Butcher, "Come along with me," and led the way out a the cell and into the back room where I splashed my face with water and picked up a dirty towel from off the table. While I was wiping my face dry, I said, "Go on ahead." Butcher dipped his hands into the bowl and rubbed water into his face. I don't know about me, 'cause I never looked in no mirrer, but when we had finished with that little ritual, ole Butcher did look somewhat better. I walked back out into the office. Happy was setting behind my desk with his big feet on the top of it.

"Happy," I said, "get your feet off a my desk."

He set up right fast real straight and looked at me with wide open eyeballs. "Yes sir," he said.

"Why don't you run on out and get yourself some breakfast," I said. "I'll be along with ole Butcher in just a little bit."

"Yes sir," he said again, and he stood up and headed on out. About the time he got the door shut behind hisself, Butcher come out into the office.

"Grab a chair," I said, and he did, setting right across the desk from me. "I got myself a plan," I said. "You see, ole Peester, the mayor of our little town, is wanting to get rid a me. Now, I done outfoxed him and got him over a barrel, so he can't fire me. There ain't no way. So the way I got it figgered, he's a trying to have me killed dead. That way, he's in the clear, and I'm out a the way. You get it?"

"Yeah," Butcher said. "It's pretty plain."

"All I got to do now is to just prove what I just told you. Then I can arrest his ass and throw it in jail and charge him with conspiring to murder a lawman, and I can have his ass locked up 'til he's too old to do any more mischief on me."

Butcher nodded his head kind a slow, and he said, "Uh-hun. Yeah. I get it."

"I think he asked you to do the dirty deed for him the other day. Am I right? All you got to do is say yeah, and I'll go get the bastard. Well? What did he talk to you about that time?"

"I can't tell you that, Barjack," he said.

"What the hell do you mean, you can't tell me?" I said.

"I guess you can't remember too well after all these years you been gone," Butcher said, "but in New York City, we got us a code we live by. We don't snitch. Not on nobody. I got to live by that code, even out here."

I stood up, likely a little fast, and I tuck me a deep breath to kind a calm my ass down some.

"But it's different out here," I said. "Hell, you're a lawman now. You got to live up to that new oath you tuck to uphold the law."

"I never took no oath," he said. "Don't you remember? You just tossed me this here badge and told me to pin it on. That's all."

"I'll give you the goddamn oath right now," I said.

"Okay," he said, "but it won't make me snitch."

"If you swear to uphold the law—"

"I ain't swearing to nothing that's retro—whatever they call it," he said.

I couldn't think a the word neither, but I knowed what he was trying to say. He was telling me that if he was to swear to something, it wouldn't mean nothing about what had happened back in the past. I knowed that. And I could tell that I wasn't getting nowhere with him along that line. I would just have to come up with something else, and that was that. I started walking around the desk.

"Come on," I said.

"You don't want me to swear to nothing?" he said.

"Naw, hell," I said. "It don't make no difference no how."

I led the way outside, and the first thing I seed was that nobody had bothered to do nothing about ole Batshit's dead body. It was still lying there in the middle a the street, and it was beginning to stink somewhat, and there was three or four stray dogs a sniffing at it. Lonnie the Geek was slinking along the sidewalk on the other side a the street, and I yelled at him. He come a walking toward me.

"Morning, Marshal," he said.

"Lonnie," I said, "go fetch ole digger to come down here and take care a that carcass before them dogs eats it up."

"Sure, Marshal," he said, and turned around and went hurrying down the street in the direction a the undertaker's parlor. I kept on a walking toward the Hooch House, and Butcher follered me. Dingle was setting at my table along with Happy and Sly. I was surprised to see Sly in there first thing in the morning. A course it weren't really first thing. It was midway through, but I was surprised to see him anyhow. I led Butcher on over and we set down.

"What the hell brings you a slumming over here?" I asked Sly.

He grinned and said, "I just thought I'd check up on you. See how things are going."

"Well," I said, "I ain't so sure. I think that pettifogging bastard mayor we got is planning to have me shot dead since he can't fire my ass no more." I give Butcher a dirty look and went on. "Only thing is, I can't prove it."

"We'll just have to keep our eyes open and take note of any strangers in town," Sly said. I seed that he was kinda eyeballing ole Butcher with curiousness.

"You done met Butcher here, didn't you?" I said. "Well, hell, he's my deppity now."

"Oh," Sly said. "That's interesting."

"Say, Widdamaker," I said, "how'd you like to pin on a badge?"

Sly smiled at me and said, "No, Barjack, I don't think so, but I'll be watching out for you just the same. You've already got two good men wearing badges anyway."

"Well, I reckon that'll have to do," I said. Happy was beaming at that, and Butcher looked pleased too.

Aubrey come out a the back room then a toting Happy's breakfast, and soon as I could get his attention, I told him to bring me and Butcher the same thing, and to bring us some coffee first. He went on back to do all that, but he brung out the coffee first. I said, "Aubrey, bring me over a tumbler a whiskey too. Anyone else?"

No one else wanted any, so Aubrey run on. Dingle was a writing in his notepad and not paying much attention to no one else. Bonnie come flouncing down the stairs just then, and she come over and set her wide ass down beside me.

"Good morning, Mr. Sly," she said with a big friendly smile, and I was thinking that son of a bitch could steal another woman from me if he was to want to. Then I told myself that he seemed to be pretty contented with just Lillian, so I ought not to worry my ass none about it. He had did me some damn good favors in the past, and I had by God better keep them in my head.

Sly touched the brim of his hat and smiled and said, "Good morning, Miss Boodle."

Then ole Bonnie spoke to ever'one else at the table, and final she looked at me and kind a sniffed, and she said, "Barjack, I'll have you a bath drawed."

"I don't need no bath," I said.

"I'll have it drawed for you," she said with a kind a icy voice, so I just kept my mouth shut. Aubrey brung out the breakfasts then, and me and Butcher went to shoveling food into our yaps. Bonnie took the opertunity to tell Aubrey to have me a bath drawed up in our room upstairs, and he said he would right away and left us again. I washed down my breakfast with the rest a my cup a coffee, and then I went to drinking my whiskey. Sly got up and excused hisself most politely-like, and then he went on his way. Happy had done finished eating.

"Barjack," he said, "what do you want me to do?"

"Just hang around, Happy," I said, "in case I should need you."

Dingle was still a scribbling. By and by ole Aubrey come over and told Bonnie that the bathwater was drawed upstairs, and Bonnie gouged me real hard in the ribs.

"Ow," I said.

"Come on, Barjack," she said, and she stood up a dragging on me at the same time. She pulled me on up to my feet and hauled my ass up the stairs. When we was in the room, she went to pulling off all a my clothes and made me climb into the tub a hot, sudsy water, which I done. Then she went to scrubbing me all over with that long-handled brush 'til I thunk that she might be scrubbing off some a my skin. When she final got did with me, she tuck hold a me again and hauled me out a the tub. She throwed a big towel around me and went to rubbing me dry, and by then all that activity around my old body had kind a roused me up, if you get my meaning.

Bonnie throwed me onto the bed, and she never got herself out a her clothes so fast in her whole life. She crawled right in on top a me and went to work, and I mean to tell you, we had us a real rolicky time there for quite a spell. Whenever we had just about wore our two asses out, we just laid there in bed for a time a feeling each other up a little from time to time. I was thinking how whenever ole Sly had stole my wife Lillian away from me, I had come out far the best on the deal. Then Bonnie got up out a the bed without no warning and went to laying me out some clean clothes. I got up and got myself dressed. Bonnie dressed herself up again.

"Let's go back downstairs and tend to business," she said, and I agreed with her. She held a arm out to her side, and I tuck it in mine, and we started walking down the hall to the head a the stairs. I looked down over the room below us, and I could see that Dingle was still setting there scribbling, and

Happy and Butcher was still sipping coffee and talking to each other. There was a pretty good crop a customers in the place by this time. We started on our way on down, and all of a sudden, I seen a slick-looking son of a bitch step out away from the bar and look up at me and Bonnie making our way down the stairs.

Before I knowed what was a happening, he had pulled out a six-gun and pointed it in my direction. My right arm was all tangled up with Bonnie's arm, and I tried to extercate it so I could defend my ass with my trusty Merwin and Hulbert, but before I could get loose, he fired a shot at me. I kinda ducked to one side, and when I did, I bumped into Bonnie, and the two of us tumbled over on the stairs, but as we was a going over, his shot nicked me on the goddamned ear. Not the ear what Lillian had already shot, but the other one.

"Goddamn," I roared, and I fell on over onto the landing on top a Bonnie, and the both of us commenced to rolling over and over on top a each other going down the stairs. Bonnie was a shrieking the whole way, and I was a cussing, and I could feel the blood running from my ear where the bullet had cut a notch out a the hangy-down part of it. We was about halfway down when I heared another shot, but a course, I couldn't see nothing as me and ole Bonnie was still a tumbling. Then the whole place got noisy with voices, and final me and Bonnie lit on the floor and only rolled over one more time.

I set up, and then Bonnie set up beside me, and I went to looking around. I seen Butcher standing up with his revolver in his hand, and I looked over to where that slick son of a bitch had been standing, and I seen him laid out on the floor. Bonnie got her ass up, and she reached out a hand to help me to my feet. I stood up and walked over to the corpus delete and looked down at it. It was dead all right.

"Does anyone know who this son of a bitch was?" I said out loud.

No one said nothing for a minute, and then Aubrey said, "He seems to be a stranger around here, Barjack."

"Happy," I said, "get his ass hauled out a here."

"Yes sir," said Happy, and he went about his business. I walked back to my table. Bonnie went to the bar for a wet towel. I set down and looked at ole Butcher.

"You done it again," I said.

"What?" he said. "What'd I do?"

"You saved my bacon," I said. "Twice now."

Bonnie come back with the wet rag and went to wiping the blood off a my neck. Dingle was scribbling faster than ever.

"I done all right?" said Butcher.

"Pardner," I said, "you done just right."

But I was wondering how the hell I was going to pin this on ole Peester.

Chapter Twelve

Well, natural, no one in Asininity knowed a goddamn thing about the dead son of a bitch. Not even Sly, who knowed just about all the gunfighters in the whole damned West, had no idee a who the bastard might could a been, and ole Butcher Doyle, he knowed professional killers from back East, but he never knowed this one neither. Hell, I made ever'one in town look at the stiff, and they all said the same thing. They shuck their heads and said, "No, Barjack, I ain't never saw him before in my whole goddamn life," or at least they said words to that there same effect. Ole Peester, he was damned certain about it, more than most a the others, and a course, that made me the more suspicious than ever before a the pettifogging bastard.

"You take a damn good look at the son of a bitch, Mr. Mayor?" I asked him with a suspicious tone in my voice and a accusing look in my eyes.

"I've already told you, Barjack," he said, "I've never seen this person before. He's not from around here. I know that."

"Just how do you know that?" I asked him.

"Because I know all of the people in our county, just as you do. Would you say that he could be from around here?"

"There might could be someone around that I ain't

never saw before," I told him. "Could be he come in from over around the county seat somewheres."

"I suppose it's possible," he said, "but I seriously doubt it. If he's from around here, then he must be a recent arrival, someone who just moved in. That does happen. It's—It's possible."

"So you ain't never laid eyeballs on this shithead?" I said.

"Goddamn it, Barjack," he said, and his face was a looking red and puffy, "how many times do I have to say it? I have never seen this—person—before. Will you never be satisfied?"

"Why, hell, yes, Your Orneriness," I said. "I'm satisfied as all hell. I ain't got nothing more to ask you about a tall."

The talk I had with ole Sly was somewhat different. Course, I was more friendlier with Sly than with ole Peester. First off I asked him if he had ever saw the dead bastard before, and he said as how he hadn't.

"Hell," I said, "I thought you knowed them all."

"All?" he said.

"Yeah," I said, "all them gunfighting types. I thought you knowed them all."

"He must be a new one," Sly said. "I've never seen him. And he wasn't very good."

"What the hell do you mean by that?" I said. "You wasn't here. You never seed him draw nor nothing. Did you?"

"No," he said, "I didn't, but he's dead, isn't he?"

Well, hell, I couldn't argue with that none. The son of a bitch was dead all right.

"He shot a notch out a my goddamned ear," I said, taking a holt of it and wiggling it at the Widdamaker.

"Do you think that was what he intended to do?" said Sly. "Nick your ear?"

"The bastard meant to kill me," I said.

"And all he did was nick your ear and then get himself killed. No, Barjack, he was an amateur. There's no doubt about it. Even so, it does mean that someone is definitely up to something."

"And that something is to get my ass blowed away," I said.

"I'll stay closer from here on until we get this all cleared up."

Well, I had been getting kind a tired a all a his jabbering, but whenever he said that last, I was sure enough glad to hear it. I had ole Happy, and Butcher had been a damn good ace in the hole for me. Now I had Sly, even though he wouldn't put on no badge, a saying that he would hang close. I felt some better on account a that. Even so, some lucky bastard could always get in a good shot before anyone around knowed that he was about to do it. I sure weren't out a the woods, not by a long shot. And come to think of it, a long shot was something to worry about too. A man what was good with a rifle could find hisself a high perch somewheres and wait his chance and take a long shot which could send me to bloody hell, and no one would even know where the shot had came from. I hurried on back over to the Hooch House from where I had been talking to Sly there in Lillian's place, and all the way I was a looking up on the balconies and the rooftops for any signs of ambushers what might be lurking up there. I was looking up too at all the men walking around on the street, making sure I knowed who they was.

I found Happy and Butcher and Dingle a setting at

my table, and I hustled my ass on over and set down with them. The place was crowded with customers, and I knowed most of them by sight. I seed two strangers, though a standing at the bar looking like cowhands. Both of them was wearing six-guns on their hips.

"Happy," I said, "see them two punchers over at the bar?"

"Yes sir," he said.

"You know them?"

He shuck his head real slow, and he said, "No sir. I ain't never seen them before."

"Go over there and take their shooters away from them and throw their ass in jail," I told him.

"Well, what for, Barjack?" he said.

"Because I said so. For toting guns in my town," I said. "Now get on about it."

He got up and walked on over to the bar to stand right behind them, and he pulled out his six-gun and then he said, "Put your hands up, boys."

The two strangers looked around right quick-like with damn surprised expressions on their faces, and they both put up their hands real fast whenever they seen the barrel of that Colt poked at them.

"What the hell?" said one.

"What's this all about?" said the other one.

"Just use two fingers, boys," said Happy, "and ease your guns out and put them on the bar." They done what he said, and then he told them to start in marching out a the place.

"Where you taking us?" the first one said.

"I'm marching your ass to the jailhouse," Happy said.

"Well, what the hell did we do?"

"You never checked in your guns," Happy said.

"It's against the law in Asininity to go around wearing guns."

"Hell, we didn't know that. We'll be glad to check them in."

"Just keep a walking," Happy said, and they went on out the door. I kept waiting for a gunshot to sound from off a one a the roofs out there, but it never. Sly come walking in just then. He come over to my table and said howdy all around. Dingle grunted something and kept on scribbling. Sly nodded toward the door where Happy had just gone out with them two strangers.

"What's that all about?" he asked.

"Couple a gun-toting strangers," I said.

"No trouble?" he said.

"I never give them a chance," I told him. "Have a drink?"

"Coffee," he said.

I waved a arm at Aubrey, and when he tuck note of it, I said to him out loud, "A whiskey and a coffee."

"Right away," he answered, and he was true to his word. He brung them both right over. Sly thanked him real kindly-like, and I just grunted and tuck me a drink. I sure as hell needed it too.

"Where the hell's Bonnie?" I asked kind a sudden, on account a I just then realized that I didn't see her nowhere. She had ought a been downstairs by that time too.

"She went back into the kitchen for something to eat," Doyle said.

"Oh," I said, some relieved. You see, it had come to me that she might could be in some danger her own self. Anyone who knowed anything about me might could know about Bonnie as well, and he might try to get at me by getting at her first. I sure as hell didn't want nothing like that happening. I was even more relieved whenever I seen her coming back out a the back room. She seen me too, and she come a bouncing on over to the table where I was a setting. I stood up and greeted her with a big ole hug, and it like to scared her to death, but whenever she got over her scared, she give me a big sloppy kiss right there in front a the whole world.

"Aw, set down, Bonnie," I said, and I set my own ass down. She set next to me like she always done. In just another few minutes, Happy come back in.

"They're locked up, Barjack," he said.

"Who?" said Bonnie. "Who's locked up?"

"Just a couple a strangers," I said. "It ain't nothing for you to worry your sweet ass about."

"What you got them in jail for?" she demanded, her voice getting some loud.

"Toting guns in town," said Happy.

"Oh," she said. "Is that all?"

"I told you it wasn't nothing to worry about," I said.

"Barjack?" said Happy.

"Whut?" I said.

"What're we going to do about them two in jail?"

"Don't worry about them," I said. "I'll go on over and question them after a while."

I tipped up my glass and drank it dry and held it up for Aubrey to see. He come and refilled it right soon.

"Barjack?" said Butcher, who had been total quiet up 'til right then.

"Whut?" I said again.

"Let me go question them two for you."

I give him a curious look. "How come?" I said.

"Well," he said, "you got a lot on your mind just

now, and I can do it. I can take care of that little thing for you. I ain't done nothing for you since you made me a deputy, only just kill that one guy. That's all. I'd like to be doing something. Some deputy work."

I had a pretty damn good idea a Butcher's notion of questioning, so I said, "Sure, pard. Go on ahead. All I want to know is did they come to town to kill me, and who it was that sent them."

Butcher grinned real big and shoved back his chair. He picked up the drink that was there in front of him and finished it off.

"Count on me, boss," he said, and he turned around and headed out a the Hooch House. I watched him go, and I was a wondering how he would do his questioning. I seen Happy a looking at me.

"You want me to go over there with him?" he asked me.

"No, Happy," I said. "I got another job for you."

"What is it?"

"I want you to take a rifle with you and get up on top a the highest building in town where you can see all the rooftops and all the second-story winders and anyplace where a man might could hide out with a long gun and wait for a chance to take a pot-shot at me. You got that?"

"Yes sir," he said, and he got up and headed out. That just left me and Bonnie and Sly and Dingle a setting there.

"Barjack," said Bonnie, "I'm skeered for you."

"Aw, pretty hips," I said, "just look around me here. I got the famous Widdamaker hisself right here at the table with me. Butcher's just down the street, and he'll be back, and then Happy's up on a roof somewheres a watching out for me. There ain't nothing for you to worry about."

I was sure as hell lying to her, on account a I can't remember being more skeered my own self. I never skeered easy whenever I was younger. I prob'ly figgered that if I was to get my ass killed, well, hell, I likely deserved it. And then, I never had nothing to lose. But now that I was getting older and richer and had my sweet Bonnie, I had a lot to lose, and I didn't want to lose it neither. And I sure as hell didn't want to get my ass bumped off by someone what ole Peester had hired to do the job.

"Barjack's right, Miss Bonnie," Sly said. "Oh, I won't lie to you. There is some danger, of course, but we're all watching out for him. I promise you. And Barjack is no pushover by himself, you know."

Well, now, that last puffed me up some to have the famous gunslinger build me up like that. I couldn't think of anyone in the whole goddamned world who could a said something good about me that it would a meant more to me at that time. Anytime for that. I just rared back in my chair and tuck a good sip a my good whiskey, but I was still thinking about ole Butcher and them two cowboys. I turned up my glass and drained it, and then I pushed back my chair and stood up.

"I'm going over to the jailhouse and check up on ole Butcher," I said.

"I'll walk along with you," said Sly, and he got up and follered me out onto the street and on down to the marshaling office. There was a chair out on the sidewalk, and when I went on inside, he just plunked his ass down on that chair and stayed out on the sidewalk. I heared them before I seed them.

I heared a smack and a groan, and I walked on over

to the cell where Butcher had opened up the door and gone inside with them two. One of them was slumped on a cot a holding his head, and Butcher was smacking the other one. He had them both bruised and bloody. It damn near made me sick to my guts, but I kept a holt a myself.

"Butcher," I said. "Hold up there."

He turned a loose a the guy he was smacking and let him drop. Then he looked around at me.

"I ain't got nothing out of them yet, Barjack," he said.

I stepped inside the cell, and the one what Butcher had just let drop looked up at me, and he sure did look like he was a begging for help.

"Marshal," he said, "we don't know what he's talking about."

"Did you come to town gunning for me?" I asked him.

"No," said the pitiful wretch. "We never. I swear it. We was just passing through, and we stopped for a drink. That's all."

"You know the lawyer Peester?" I asked.

"Never heard of him."

"Where'd you come from?"

"Up in the Dakotas."

"Where you headed?"

"We thought about Texas on account of it ain't so damn cold down there."

"If I was to decide to turn you a loose," I said, "would you pick up your six-shooters and ride on out a town?"

"Faster'n you can say it."

"And you won't never see us again," said the other one what had been quiet since I come in.

"Come on with me," I said, and I led the two of

them back into the back room and showed them the basin a water on the table. "Wash your faces," I said. I left them there and went back into the office where Butcher had come out a the cell by then.

"You going to let them go?" he asked me.

"They're harmless," I said. I could see that he was disappointed, so I decided to try to cheer him up some. I said, "If they'd a been after my ass, you'd a got it out of them for sure." He looked a little better then.

Chapter Thirteen

Well, things got kind a crazy after that. It were just a couple a days later whenever I was just about to leave the office when I seed ole Sly across the street in front a Lillian's fancy eating house. I guess he had just come out, and a character on a black horse a wearing a black suit and hat come riding down the street and pulled up right there in front of him. I stood still and watched. You know, I had became real suspicious and nervous-like regarding the entering into my town a strangers. Well, that stranger swung down out a his saddle and tipped his hat to Sly, and then in a loud and strong voice, I heared him say, "Howdy. I'm a stranger in town." Sly nodded him a greeting, and the stranger went on like this here. "I'm looking for the town marshal. Barjack. Can you tell me where to find him?"

"I might be able to do that," Sly said, "but first, may I ask your business?"

"My business is with Barjack," the man said. "You going to tell me where I can find him?"

"Not unless you give me more information," Sly said, and I seed that stranger's right hand brush back his coattails to free up his shooter for a quick draw. I wondered who the hell he might be.

"I asked you real polite, mister," the son of a bitch said.

"And I responded with politeness," said Sly. "If you'll tell me what you want, I might tell you where to find the marshal. Otherwise you can just continue on your way."

"What's your name?" said the stranger.

"I'm Herman Sly."

"Well, I'll be damned," said the damned fool. "The famous Widowmaker. Right?"

"I've been called that," Sly said.

"Be a feather in my hat if I take you first."

"If," said Sly. "That little bitty word carries a lot of meaning. Are you feeling lucky today?"

"Luck rides the trail with me, gunslinger," the man said, and his right hand went flashing for his shooter, and it was real fast. I was a watching him and not watching Sly, and I seldom seed a gun come out as fast as that one done. But what was even more amazing was the next thing I seed and heared. I heared a blast, but it never come from the fast gun in the goddamned stranger's hand. It come from Sly's six-gun, and it sent a slug right smack into the stranger's chest. It knocked him over on his back and he just sprawled out there deader'n a squashed bug. He never moved no more. Ole One-shot Sly done him in right there in front a me.

Well, I walked on out and across the street, and Sly seed me coming. I never let on that I had been watching the whole damn business, and when I come up on him, I looked down at the corpus and tuck note that I had never before seed the son of a bitch in my lifetime. "That was fast shooting, Sly," I said. "What the hell was it all about?"

"He came to town to kill you," Sly said.

"No shit?" I said.

"He didn't exactly say so," Sly told me, "but he

asked for you. When I refused to accommodate him, he asked my name. I told him, and then he said that it would be a feather in his cap if he killed me first. His meaning was pretty clear, I think."

"Well, goddamn, I would say so," I said. "Hey, do you know who the hell the dead bastard is—or was?"

"I never met him before," Sly said, "but I think I know who he is. I've heard about a young comer called Stokes. This man's looks and attitude match what I've heard."

"Stokes, huh? Well, we can put that on his marker with a question mark after it. Come on down to the Hooch House and let me buy you a drink. Course, we'll never know now, but you might just could a saved my life, ole pard."

Sly walked on down to the Hooch House with me, and he actual let me buy him a drink. Course, we found Dingle and Happy and Bonnie all a setting at my table, and a course, I had my usual tumbler full a good brown whiskey.

"I heard a gunshot, Barjack," said Happy.

"I notice that you never hurried on out into the street to do no investigating," I said.

"I was fixing to," he said, "but then you come walking on in here, so I thought I'd just wait and see what you had to say about it."

"Is that right?" I said.

"Yes sir," Happy said. "Hell, I was just damn near up and out a my chair when you come in."

"What if someone had a kilt me?" I said.

"Well, we'd a got him for you," said Happy. "Me and Butcher and ole Sly here. We'd a got him."

"That wouldn't a helped me out none, now would it? Say, where is Butcher?"

"He said something about getting a bath," said Bonnie. "Now what the hell was that gunshot?"

"Oh, that," I said. "Hell, it weren't nothing much. Ole Sly here just killed a man."

"Who was it?" said Dingle, looking up from his scribbling with wide eyes.

"We ain't sure," I said. "We think it was some little ole fart name of Stokes or something like that."

"Well," Dingle said, "why did Mr. Sly shoot him?"

I kind a shrugged and picked up my glass to have a drink. "I ain't sure," I said. "He must a said something what rubbed ole Sly the wrong way."

Bonnie slapped me on the shoulder so damn hard she like to knocked me over onto the floor. The legs a my chair what was closest to her got raised right up off a the floor.

"Barjack," she yelled at me, "what was it all about?"

"The man came to town to kill Barjack, Miss Boodle," said Sly.

"Oh," she kind a shrieked.

"The only thing is," I added to the story, "the damn fool decided to try to kill ole Sly here first."

I laughed out loud like that was the funniest thing I had heared in a good long while, and it damn near was too. If the dead ignorant bastard had any brains a tall, he'd a killed me first and then gone on to kill Sly. That way he at least had a chance a getting his job did before he went on to hell. Sly grinned a little out a politeness to me, I guess, but no one else seed it funny the way I seed it. I shut up and drank some more a my whiskey. Just then ole Butcher Doyle come a walking in all dressed up in fresh, clean clothes and looking like as if he was a fixing to go out on the town back in New York City. He come over and set down, and he went and asked about the gunshot, which he had heared too. Well, we told the story again, and then I said, "It's a fine goddamned mess whenever some son of a bitch rides into town to kill my ass, and one goddamn depitty is taking hisself a bath and the other one is setting at my own table and drinking my goddamn whiskey."

"A man's got to have a bath ever' now and then," said Butcher, with a pout on his face.

"And you," I said to Happy. "I thought I tole you to set up on a roof and watch things from up yonder for me."

"Well, that's right, Barjack," he said. "You did tell me to do that, but I was just taking a little break. That's all."

"Well, get your ass back up there," I said. "Hell, someone could kill me while you're taking a break. Goddamn it."

Happy got up and left the Hooch House looking kind a like a whipped pup, and Butcher just set there looking more or less the same way. I waved at Aubrey and had him fetch Butcher a drink. That made him feel a little better, I guess. In another minute, Happy come back in. I give him a hell of a look.

"Barjack?" he said.

"Whut?" I said. "What the hell is it now?"

"If I was to see a stranger ride into town," he asked me, "what do I s'posed to do to let you know about it?"

"Hell, Happy," I said, "just shoot the son of a bitch."

"Okay," he said, and he walked out the front door again. Sly give me a questioning look.

"Just shoot him?" he said.

I just shrugged and drank down some more

whiskey. Well, from then on whenever it come time for meals and such, I had ole Butcher go up on top and take Happy's place for a spell. Things went on like that for a couple a days or so, and then one afternoon, I was setting in the Hooch House having a drink with my Bonnie. Weren't no one else in there with us at just that time. I don't know where the hell they was all at, but I figgered that Happy was on his rooftop, but I don't where the others was at. Well, setting there just me and ole Bonnie, I got to feeling a little randy, you know, and I put my hand on her knee and let it slide kind a easy-like on up her leg and even under her skirt a little, and I said, "Sugar tits, let's you and me go upstairs for a little while. What do you say?"

"Well, honey," she said, "let's just us do that."

So we got up and headed for the stairs. We held on to each other on the way up and on down the hall to our room. Inside I pulled off my coat and tossed it aside. Then I went to hauling my boots off, and Bonnie was about to wiggle out a her dress when she noticed that the whiskey bottle in our room was damn near empty. "Barjack," she said. "You reckon I should call ole Aubrey and have him bring us another bottle up here?"

I looked over at the empty, and I said, "Yeah. Sure." Bonnie went out into the hallway, and I hauled off my second boot and tossed it on the floor. I stood up and shrugged out a my vest and my shirt, and then it come into my head that I didn't want ole Aubrey coming up to the room, so I padded out into the hallway in just my sock feet. Bonnie was just at the head a the stairs, and there was two rough-looking bastards I hadn't never seed before coming up, just about to meet her. She stopped.

"What the hell do you want up here?" she said.

The men stopped right close to the top step. One a them touched the brim of his hat, and he said, "Why, ma'am, we just come up here looking for the marshal."

"Someone told us he was up here," the other one said.

Without no warning, Bonnie swung both a her arms up and caught both a them bastards just under the chin. They yowled and went over bass-akwards, a tumbling and bouncing over each other all the way back down to the main floor. I run over to beside Bonnie, and I hauled out my Merwin and Hulbert. I hadn't yet unbuckled my gun belt. And I commenced to follering them two down the stairs. I was holding my shooter ready for action. Whenever they hit the floor, they stopped rolling, a course, and one of them just lay still. The other'n started in trying to get his ass up off the floor.

"Just set there quiet-like," I said to him, and he set still a holding his head. Bonnie come a bouncing down the stairs behind me. She stopped beside me and put a hand on my shoulder.

"Who are they?" she said.

"I never seed them before," I said.

Bonnie of a sudden swung out her right foot and kicked that poor son of a bitch right up beside a the head.

"Just who the hell are you?" she roared at him.

He set up again and was holding his head in his hands. "Never mind kicking him," I said. "Get their guns."

Bonnie stepped on down onto the floor and walked around behind him and leaned over to pull the six-gun out a his holster. Then she went over to the other one, who still had not moved, and she bent over him and got his gun out. "Go put them on the bar," I said, and she did.

"Now," I said to the kicked bastard, "what's your name?"

He looked up at me but he never said nothing.

"You want me to give you another swift kick?" I asked him. "I kick some harder than the lady there." Course, I sure as hell did not kick harder than ole Bonnie, and I weren't about to kick his hard head nohow with just only my foot without no boot on it, but I never let on to none a that.

"Name's Holbrook," he said.

"What about your pard there?" I said.

"Crawford," he said.

"Holbrook and Crawford," I said, but neither one a them names rang no bells.

"I think he's dead," Holbrook said.

"Then he won't mind waiting a spell," I said. "What was you two doing here a looking for me?"

"We, uh, we wanted to report something to you," he said.

"Okay," I said. "Get to reporting."

"Well, I, uh, I can't think straight right now," he said. "Getting knocked down them stairs. My partner's laying there dead."

Bonnie come back just then, and she said, "Can't think, huh? S'pose I slap the shit out a you."

"You already done that, honey britches," I said. "Just let me handle this now. You know what I think?" I said back to Holbrook. "I think you two come to town to try and kill me."

"No," said Holbrook. "Why, I don't even know you. Neither did poor ole Crawford there. We didn't know you."

"That means that you was hired to do the job then," I said. "Who's doing the hiring?" He never answered me. "Who's paying you?" I said. He still kept his yap shut, and just then ole Butcher come a walking into the place. When he seed what was going on, he come right on over.

"Butcher," I said, "where the hell you been?"

"Why, I was just—"

"Never mind," I said. "Take this son of a bitch over to the jailhouse and lock his ass up. And have someone carry this other dead one out a here."

"Yes sir, boss," he said, and he grabbed Holbrook by his collar and pulled him up to his feet, and right away started in to marching him out a the place. I let the two a them get out the front door before I holstered my ole Merwin and Hulbert again. Then I leaned on the rail there and heaved out a heavy sigh. I tell you what. I was getting goddamn fed up with all that shit. Hell. A man a my age.

"You should a killed him, Barjack," Bonnie said.

"Hell, babe," I said, "there's witnesses in here. I couldn't a just shot him dead and him without no gun in his hand."

"But he come in here to kill you," she said.

"I ain't got no proof a that," I said. "Don't worry none. Maybe he'll try to break out a jail or something. Anyhow, I'd like to find out for sure who it was that paid them two to blow my ass away."

"How you going to do that?" she said.

I just kind a smiled. I didn't say nothing, but I was thinking about ole Butcher and his special ways a questioning prisoners. I just set right down there on the steps in my half undressed condition to wait for Butcher to get back so I could turn him a loose on that Holbrook.

Chapter Fourteen

Well, I tuck ole Bonnie back upstairs and we got it on. I was turned on real good by then on account a my sweet hips had done broke a man's neck for me. It was damn fine, I tell you. Then I got me cleaned up a little and got my clothes back on and strutted my ass right back on down to my table, waving at Aubrey as I went by. Butcher was setting there with a drink, and Dingle was setting there scribbling. I reckoned that ole Happy was on a rooftop somewheres. I set my ass down, and I guess I was just a beaming. Aubrey brung my tumbler over full a whiskey.

"I locked him up, Barjack," Butcher said.

"Good," I said.

"And I got that other'n taken down to the undertaker's parlor."

"Good again," I said. I tuck me a swaller a good whiskey. "Butcher," I said, "do you know what happened here?"

"No," he said. "I come in too late to see it, and you never told me. You just told me to take that one to jail and get the other one hauled off. I—"

"I know," I said. "I know. Well, let me tell you. I was upstairs with my Bonnie. I reckon you seed how I was just only half-dressed."

"Yeh," he said. "I seen that."

"Well, Bonnie, she was fixing to come back down

here to fetch up a fresh bottle a good brown whiskey, and she met them two at the head a the stairs. They said they was looking for me. Well, she knocked both their asses plumb down the stairs. Yes sir. She whopped them both at one time and sent them flying. Goddamn, that's a hell of a woman, ain't it? There just ain't none like my sweet-ass Bonnie Boodle. No sir. And that ain't the first time she's saved my ass, Butcher. Did you know that. By God, she'd kill a man for me. What the hell am I saying? She has kilt a man for me. More than once. 'Course, I got to watch my ass. If I was to piss her off, she'd kill me too. Just as quick. She's a hell of a woman."

Well, I shut up of a sudden. I couldn't recollect another time I had talked so damn much. I tuck a big slug a whiskey and tried to figger out just what had got into me to make me jabber on like that. I had just had me a fine piece a tail, but it sure as hell weren't the first time for that. Bonnie had just before that broke a bastard's neck for me, but she had kilt for me before too. Then it come to me that it must a been my nerviness all messed up with them other two things. I weren't sure, and I still ain't. I guess it never really mattered none, except only it kind a embarrassed me that I had let my tongue flap so much just then.

"Butcher," I said.

"Yeh?"

I guess I ain't mentioned it yet, but ole Butcher Doyle, he had a real strong and peculiar New York way a talking which I hadn't tried to even imitate by my spelling or nothing. He said things like "dis" and "dat" 'stead of "this" and "that." And he said "earl" for "oil." I had got my ass out a New York City young enough that I had got over whatever New York way a talking I had growed up with, but ole Butcher, his way a talking sure as hell did stand out around Asininity. I was kind a worried that it might could start to rub off on me.

"Butcher," I said, "how'd you like to do some more interrogating?"

"You mean question that bastard in the jail?" he said.

"That's just exact what I mean," I said. "I need to know just who the hell was it what paid them two bastards to kill me. Go see if you can't find out for me."

Butcher grinned real wide and got up out a his chair. "I'll ask him," he said.

"Ask him real nice," I said.

His grin got even wider, and he said, "Yes sir. I'll ask him real nice." He walked on out a the Hooch House with a real jaunty kind a step. Dingle was still scribbling, and Bonnie come down the stairs just then. She was smiling and her tits was bouncing real nice. I reckon she felt about as good about knocking them two down the stairs as I felt about her a doing it. She waved at Aubrey on the way and then come right on over to the table and set down beside me.

"Bonnie, sweet ass," I said, "you outdone yourself today. That was just wonderful the way you busted them two."

She kind a giggled and wiggled around on her ass and snuggled up against me. Dingle scribbled faster. Happy come in just then, and he come over to set with us.

"Where was you?" I asked him.

"I was on the roof, where you told me to be," he said.

"I had you up there to warn me when strangers was a coming into town," I said. "How'd them two get in here? Tell me that."

"I seen them ride in," Happy said, "but whenever I could tell they was strangers, they had done turned their horses up to the rail where I couldn't get a good shot at them. Then it took me a spell to get down off a the roof."

"It damn sure did," I said. "It tuck you long enough that them two got their ass dismounted, got their horses tied, come into the Hooch House, found out somehow that I was upstairs, and then went and made their goddamn way all the way to the top a the stairs, and they'd a by God kilt my ass if it hadn't a been for ole Bonnie here."

"Bonnie?" said Happy, and he give her a look.

"Yeah, Bonnie," I said. "She met the bastards at the top a the stairs and knocked their ass plumb back down here to the floor. Kilt one of them dead, she did. She saved my ass for sure."

"Well, that's just amazing, Miss Bonnie," Happy said, giving her a wide-eyed admiring kind a look. Bonnie grinned and turned a little bit red in her round face and ducked her head.

I never did get back to the subject a Happy neglecting his duties up on the damn roof, and he sure as hell never brung it back up. I was kind a anxious about Butcher's questioning a that prisoner, so I drunk up my whiskey and made my excuse and got up to leave the Hooch House. In another couple a minutes, I was down at the marshaling office and inside, and I heared right away the smacking a Butcher's fists on that bastard's face and head.

"Who you working for?" Butcher said.

"I don't know what you're talking about," the bastard said.

Whop! Butcher hit him again. I was inside by then and watching the show. The bastard fell back on the cot and banged his head against the wall. Butcher stepped up quick-like and slapped him hard across the both sides a his face.

"Who?" he said.

"No one," said the other one.

Butcher grabbed him up by the shirtfront clean up on his feet again, and then he drave a hard right hand into the bastard's gut what doubled him over and tuck away all a his air. While he was still a gasping for some breath, Butcher banged him up beside the head. The son of a bitch fell over onto the floor, and Butcher commenced to kicking at him in the ribs and the head. I noticed that ole Butcher was breathing real hard. He had been at it for a spell.

"Butcher," I said. "Take a break."

Butcher kind a straightened up his shirt, give a last kick to the bastard's ribs, and stepped out a the cell. He shut the door and locked it and walked over to the chair on the front side a my desk and set his ass down in it. I was back behind the desk already by that time, and I had done opened the drawer. I brung out two glasses and my bottle and poured us each a drink. I shoved one glass across the desk toward ole Butcher, and he tuck it. I picked mine up and lifted it, and he lifted his, and then we drank.

"The son of a bitch won't talk, huh?" I said.

"I'll make the bastard talk," Butcher said. He tuck a drink a his whiskey, and I did too, a drink a mine, that is. Then I stood up, taking my glass with me, and I walked over to the cell and looked through the bars at the poor bloody bastard. He had crawled up onto his hands and knees and was trying to get his ass up onto the cot. He looked over and seed me.

"You son of a bitch," he said, and when he talked, he spit out blood.

"Hell," I said, "I never done that to you."

"Fuck you," he said.

"I never even throwed you down the stairs," I said. "I ain't laid a hand on you. It was you and your pard what was fixing to kill me. If anyone was mad at anyone else it had ought to be me being mad at you. But I ain't mad at you."

I was lying, a course. Really I would a liked to a gone in that cell and finished up what ole Butcher had started, but I had me a plan. I meant to sort a make friends with the feller. Well, not exactly friends, but I meant to kind a play it friendly-like with him where maybe he would talk to me rather than get ole Butcher back in there on his ass. Back behind me, ole Butcher drained his glass and stood up. He walked over to the cell to stand by me, and he said, "I'm rested up enough, Barjack. Let me at him again."

"No, Butcher," I said. "You go on and get yourself something to eat. I'll stick around here for a spell. Go on now."

He give a shrug and went on out a the office.

"Looks like he hurt you pretty bad," I said.

"Fuck him," he said.

"You got a big vocabalary, friend," I said. He hacked and coughed and spit some blood out onto the floor. "Holbrook," I said. "Here. You look to me like you just might need some a this." I shoved my glass, which was still about half-full a good whiskey, through the bars. He looked up me suspicious-like. "Ain't nothing wrong with it," I said, and I tipped it up and tuck me another drink out of it. I pushed it back through the bars. He stood up then on weak legs and come over to the bars, and he tuck that glass out a my hand, and he drunk hisself a big swaller. "That better?" I asked him. He never answered. He just tuck another swaller.

He made his way on back over to the cot, toting my tumbler along with him, and set his ass down on it right heavy-like. "If I get out a here alive," he said, "I mean to kill that goddamned deputy of yours."

"Well, now," I said, "that's interesting, on account a you come here meaning to kill me too. Ain't that right?"

He just tuck another drink.

"I wish you'd talk to me," I said. "I wish you'd tell me what it is I want to know. I hate to let ole Butcher in here with you again, but I can't hardly control his ass when he gets a notion in his head. Only thing is, I ain't sure how much more a that you can take."

"I can take as much as he can dish out," Holbrook said.

"I ain't so sure a that," I said. "You ever hear about the Five Points Gang?"

He give me a queer look. "They don't operate around here," he said.

"You're goddamn right about that," I said. "They run New York City. They're the meanest, toughest bunch a bastards you never thunk about in your whole damn life. And that's where ole Butcher comes from. He's one a them."

"New York City, huh?" Holbrook said. "I thought he talked funny."

"You tell him that and see what happens," I said.

"I'll tell him all right," Holbrook said. "Right to his ugly fucking face. I'll tell him all right."

"You got some kind a death wish or something?" I asked him.

"I ain't talking," he said, "not to you or to him."

I shrugged like as if it didn't make no difference to me, and I headed back over to my desk. "Well, that's too bad for you," I said. "Too bad for me too on account a it makes more work for me." I set down behind the desk.

"What the hell do you mean?" he said.

"I got to figger out how to justify it on paper whenever they find you in your cell all beat to death," I said. "And that ain't easy. No sir. They don't like it when a prisoner gets his ass beat to death right there in his cell."

I tuck out some paper and a pencil and done my best imitation a ole Dingle at scribbling. I weren't really writing nothing. I was just making little marks, but I sure enough did wrinkle up my face like I was thinking real hard.

"Barjack," Holbrook said.

I looked up and toward the cell. He was standing at the cell door and holding my tumbler out through the bars at me.

"Can I have some more?" he said. He sure did look pitiful, and I damn near felt some sorry for him. I picked up the bottle and walked over to the cell and poured him another glassful. Then I walked back to the desk and set back down. I never looked up at him again. I was wanting to look as if I didn't really give much of a shit about what he said or done. I went back to my scribbling and scratching a my head. Well, it didn't take long before I was bored and tired a the faking, and I got up to leave the marshaling office.

"Barjack," Holbrook said, just as I was fixing to

open the door to leave. I looked back at him. "You just leaving me here like that?" he said.

"I might just as well," I said. "You ain't going to talk to me."

"No," he said. "I ain't."

I walked on out the door and headed back for the Hooch House. As I went inside, ole Happy jumped up from where he was a setting at my table and started to hurry his way toward the door. I stopped him.

"What's your hurry, Happy?" I asked him.

"I got to get back up on the roof," he said.

I pondered how them two had got into town in spite of Happy being posted up there, and I said, "Just forget it."

"What?" he said.

"Forget about setting up on the roof," I said. "You didn't do no good up there nohow. Come on back and set down again."

He follered me back to the table. Butcher was there and Dingle and Bonnie. We set down and called for fresh drinks.

"Did he talk?" Butcher asked me.

"Hell, no," I said. "All he said was that he meant to kill you whenever he gets out a there. And that you got a ugly fucking face."

Butcher's face set hard and for damn sure ugly at that. He kind a ground his teeth, and he shoved his chair back away from the table and stood up fast, tall and straight as he could manage.

"Where you going?" I said.

"I'm going back to work, Barjack," he said.

I never even tried to stop him. He turned toward the front door and headed out.

"What's he mean, Barjack?" Happy asked me.

"It sounded clear enough to me," I said. "He's going back to work."

"I mean, what's he going to do?"

"I guess he's going back to the marshaling office and question that prisoner some more. The man's stubborn as hell. He just won't tell us nothing."

"Should I go help him?" Happy said.

"No, Happy, just set tight. Keep close to me in case I need you. Butcher don't need no help."

Dingle kept scribbling, but he said out a the side of a silly grin on his mouth, "Barjack doesn't need any help either, as long as Bonnie's here."

Chapter Fifteen

It was the next day, and I was just a walking down the street when I seen a rough looking hombre standing kind a in my path and grinning at me. I stopped walking and stared back at him. It were yet another one. I could damn sure tell it. "You looking for me, are you?" I asked him.

"You're Marshal Barjack, ain't you?" he said.

"I reckon I am. What's your business with me?"

"I mean to shoot you dead," he said. "Go for your gun."

"How come you mean to shoot me dead?" I said. "I don't reckon I can ever recall having seed you before this."

"I got my reasons," he said. "Go for it."

"Who sent you, you cheap son of a bitch?"

"I said go for it, Barjack."

Just then ole Sly stepped up right beside me, and the bastard what was trying to shoot it out with me went to looking at Sly.

"John Mortimer," Sly said. "Fancy seeing you here."

"You keep out a this, Sly," said this feller Mortimer. "This is between me and Barjack. It ain't your business."

"I'm making it my business," Sly said. "Now, you go for your gun."

"I know you," Mortimer said. "You never draw first, so if I don't draw, you won't."

While Mortimer was busy with all a his attention on ole Sly, I just kind a turned my back on the whole thing, and I slipped my Merwin and Hulbert out a the holster, and then I slipped my right hand, which was a holding it under the left side a my coat. Then I turned halfway back around, so that I was standing with my left side toward Mortimer and my six-gun, under my coat, aimed right at the son of a bitch.

"Never mind, Sly," I said. "I'll take the bastard."

"I swore to look out for you, Barjack," Sly said.

"Stay out of it," I said.

"I ain't going to try to shoot you with him standing right there," Mortimer said.

"Walk on over to the sidewalk, Sly," I said.

Sly kind a give a shrug and walked off to the side.

"Go for it, goat shit," I said.

Mortimer reached fast for his shooter, and I pulled the trigger underneath my coat. It blowed a hole in my good coat and right on into Mortimer's chest. His shooter was just only about halfway out. He had a hell of a surprised look on his face. He just stood still for a couple a seconds, and then he tuck two staggering steps backward, and then he kind a crumpled up there in the street. Just then Happy and Butcher come a running to see what the shooting was all about. I tole Happy to take care a the corpus and Butcher to pick up the six-gun and take it on over to the marshaling office. Sly come walking back over beside me.

"You hauled that shooter out real quick," he said.

"Yeah," I said, dropping it back into my holster. Sly tuck hold a my coat by the left side and raised it up a little, and he poked his finger through the hole

I had just made. I looked him in the face, and he just kind a grinned at me. Then he let go a my coat, and asked me, "Do you want a drink?"

"You goddamned right," I said, and the two of us headed for the Hooch House. Bonnie was standing just outside the door. She had heared the shot too and had come out to see what she could see.

"Barjack?" she said.

"It's all right, sugar tits," I said. "It's all over and did with."

We went on inside and tuck our usual places and Aubrey fetched us over our drinks. Bonnie tuck a quick slug a hers, and then she said, "Another one, Barjack?"

"You still got some left in your glass, sweetness and light," I said.

"That ain't what I meant," she snarled at me. "I meant was that another gunfighter trying to kill you?"

"It was, "I said, "but he never got the job did. Hell, he never even cleared his holster."

"Did Mr. Sly get him?" she asked.

"Barjack got him," Sly said. "I went out there to help, but he wouldn't have any of it. Drilled him clean."

Ole Bonnie glommed onto my arm real tight, and looked up into my face a grinning, and went to wiggling around 'til I was a skeered she might break the legs a her chair. "Those goddamned bastards better learn not to mess with my Barjack," she said.

Happy and ole Butcher come back in just then, and just as they was a walking up to the table, Happy asked, "Another stranger?"

"I knew him," said Sly. "His name was John Mortimer, and he was a notorious professional killer."

"Good thing you were there, Mr. Sly," Happy said.

"I didn't do a thing," Sly said.

Happy and Butcher both looked at me then, and Happy said, "You done it?"

"Is it that goddamn hard to believe?" I said.

"Well, no, I just—"

"Remember the goddamned Bensons and all them others?"

"Yeah. I do, but—"

"Set down and shut up and order yourself a drink," I said. My two hotshot depitties set their asses down, and Happy waved at Aubrey. He brung them drinks. He looked at my glass and at Bonnie's, and then he brung us each some more. Right then ole Dingle come a running in, and he set down fast and slapped his silly little notepad on the table in front of him.

"What happened?" he said. "What did I miss?"

Sly went and told him the whole story, but only he left out the part about me having my gun out and under my coat. Dingle wrote as fast as ever he could.

"I'm getting goddamned tired of this bullshit," I said.

"What, Barjack, honey?" Bonnie asked me.

"I'm sick unto death a all these bastards coming into town with the full intent a doing my ass in. How goddamn long is it going to go on anyhow? 'Til I'm dead or Peester's dead?"

"Barjack?" said Butcher.

"Whut?"

"I went back and questioned that man in jail again."

"What'd you find out?"

"Well, he never would admit to even knowing the mayor."

"Hell, I figgered that much," I said.

"No sir," Butcher went on. "He claimed to be fronting for some other fellas."

"Whut?" I said. "Other fellas? Who the hell?"

"He said there was two of them," ole Butcher told me. "One was named Marlin, and the other one was named Martin. Ain't that something? Marlin and Martin?"

Well, I sure as hell scruntched up my face at that on account a it did bring back some old memories to me. But I didn't want to jump to no conclusions.

"Just Marlin and Martin?" I said. "Did he tell you nothing else? Any more names?"

"No, just them two, but then, he did call their first names. Sort of. He called one Jug."

"Jug," I said.

"And he called the other one Snake Eyes."

"Snake Eyes," I said.

"Barjack," said Sly. "Could he be talking about the old Snake Eyes gang? The Snake Eyes Kid?"

"Snake Eyes Marlin," I said, "and his little brother Jug what changed his name to Jug Martin."

"He changed his name from Jug Marlin to Jug Martin?" Bonnie said. "That don't seem too bright."

"Brightness is one thing that ole Jug weren't never accused of," I said. Then I looked back at ole Butcher what had set down by then, and I said, "So that ole boy we got in the jailhouse said he was fronting for Snake Eyes?"

"Yes sir. That's what he said when he couldn't take no more, uh, questioning."

Well, that sure as hell set me to thinking for real and for sure. Ole Snake Eyes sure as hell did have some real good reasons for wanting to get my ass killed, but it was just that I hadn't give him a thought for several years. I had kilt a number a his gang members. I had shot up his little brother's arm real bad. I had kept him from getting his claws on some stoled bank money, and then, to top it all off, I had got him sent off to jail for a good long spell a cooling off.

"Happy," I said, "run down to ole Simp's office and send off a wire to the state pen. Ask them when Snake Eyes got out."

"Yes sir," Happy said, and he got up right fast and headed for the door.

But I went on thinking. It suddenly come to me that if it was ole Snake Eyes what was trying to get me kilt, that I just might a been doing that pettifogging bastard Peester a real serious disservice. Still, I couldn't afford to be taking no chances. I shoved back my chair and stood up.

"I'll be back in a while," I said.

"Where you going, Barjack?" Bonnie said.

"Never mind," I said. "I'll be back."

I walked down to my marshaling office and went inside. Holbrook was sagging on the cot. He was bloody all over. Ole Butcher had damn sure worked him over real good. I walked up to the cell door and stood looking at him for a spell. Final, he looked up at me. My God but his face was a mess.

"Holbrook," I said.

"What? Ain't you done enough to me?"

"I ain't done nothing to you," I said. "That was my depitty. He's new, and he's real anxious to make a good impression on me. You should ought to be able to understand that."

Holbrook made a noise like "humph" and ducked his head again to look down at the floor between his feet.

"My depitty tells me that you was working for ole Snake Eyes Marlin. Is that the goddamned truth?"

"I said it once," Holbrook said. "No reason to deny it now."

"Where did you see the son of a bitch?" I asked him. "Or when?"

"I never seen him. An ole boy named Hatch come to see me and made the offer. He had just got out of the place. He knowed Snake Eyes in there."

I figgered that I had got all out of ole Holbrook that I could, so I left there and went on over to Peester's office and just barged my ass right on in. Peester weren't too happy to see me none.

"What is it, Barjack?" he said.

"Do you remember ole Snake Eyes Marlin?" I asked him.

"No," he said. "Oh, yeah. Right. Didn't he come through here a few years ago? You arrested him and his brother. I think they got sent up to the pen."

"That's right," I said. "You seed or heared anything a him since then?"

"No. Why?"

"Never mind about that," I said. "I just mainly come over here to tell you that I got that little book wrote up and printed. You know. The one I tole you about. I ain't showed it to no one. I packaged up all the copies and give them to a friend of mine. Someone I can really trust."

"Who?" Peester said, jumping up out a his chair. "Who has the book?"

"Well, now, Your Holiness," I said, "don't you worry your ass none about that. I'll just tell you that ain't no one going to see it, only if something should happen to me. I hope you get my meaning all right."

I left Peester's office without saying nothing else and headed back for the Hooch House. Ever'one was still just a setting there. I waved at Aubrey and went on back to my chair and set. Aubrey brung me my drink. Ever'one at my table was a staring at me, looking like as if they wanted me to fill them in on what I done. Final ole Bonnie, who most likely had the least patience a anyone there, spoke up.

"All right, Barjack," she said in a loud voice, "tell us. Where the hell did you go and what the hell did you do?"

"We are just a little curious, Barjack," said Sly.

Well, I rared back in my chair and tried to look my most pompous, and I give a couple of ahems to kind a clear my throat, and then final I decided to fill them all in.

"Well," I said, "I went over to the jailhouse and had me a little talk with that Holbrook feller what ole Butcher had done questioned for me, and I asked him about his dealings with ole Snake Eyes. He went and confirmed what Depitty Doyle had done found out and told me. So I went on over to Peester's office. He remembered Snake Eyes all right, but he claimed that he hadn't seed nothing nor heared nothing about him for years."

"You didn't believe the lying son of a bitch, did you?" said Bonnie.

"Well, now, sweetness," I said, "I ain't sure, but I think I do believe him. But that don't matter none really, on account a I fixed his clock real good. I got something hanging over his head now that g'arantees that he won't bother me no more."

"Are you sure about that, Barjack?" Sly asked me.

"As sure as I can be about anything," I said. Just then Happy come running back in and said that he had sent that wire on for me. "What we got to watch out for now, I'm pretty goddamn sure, is that son of a bitching bastard Snake Eyes and his little fucking brother Jug Marlin or Jug Martin, whichever he's a calling hisself these days."

"I remember them two," said Happy. "I'll sure as hell keep a eye out for them all right."

"I know Snake Eyes," said Sly. "I ran across him some years ago during a range war in Wyoming."

"Was you and him pards?" I asked.

"We were on opposite sides, Barjack," Sly said.

"I'm glad to hear that," I said.

"So what do we do now, boss?" ole Butcher said.

"Well," I started to say, but just then I seed ole Simp a coming in the front door with a paper in his hand, and he come right at me too, so I just shut up and waited for him. He hurried over and handed me the paper, and he said, "This just come in, Barjack. Do you want me to wait?" I looked over the paper, which was the answer to my wire, and I said, "No, Simp, get your ass on back to work."

"Well?" said Bonnie.

"This here says that they just only let them two brothers out a the jug a couple a days ago. That kind a confirms ole Holbrook's story."

"You mean," said Sly, "that Snake Eyes was sending killers out to get you while he was still incarcerated, but now—"

"Now that he's out," I said, "I reckon he'll be coming to town his own self."

Chapter Sixteen

Well, now, my whole entire focus was done all changed around. I weren't looking out no more for strangers what was sent by Peester. Matter a fact, I didn't believe no more that I would even have to watch out for no more strangers a tall. Hell, maybe ole Peester had sent the first one or two after me, but I had him pure damn buffaloed now. I wasn't no more worried about him than about a pissant. What I figgered now was that ole Snake Eyes had sent some men out to get me, but now that he had done been turned a loose, he would be coming his own self to have the pure pleasure of blowing my ass away. I told Happy and Butcher to watch my town for me on account a I had some important business over at the county seat.

"Well, Barjack," Happy said, "you for sure you don't want at least one of us to ride along with you what with that Snake Eyed son of a bitch trying to hunt you down?"

"You cut out trying to think, Happy," I said. "Just do what the hell I tole you to do and that's all."

"Yes sir," he said.

I done had my horse all packed up and ready to ride, and it was tied up out in front a the marshaling office. I had done tole Bonnie I was going, so I headed on out, but just when I stepped out the front door a the office, ole Sly, he come riding up on his horse. He hauled up right there beside mine, and he said, "Going for a ride, Barjack?"

"Just over to the county seat," I said.

"Could you stand some company?"

"Goddamn right," I said.

I clumb up on the back a my nag and swung it around in the right direction. Sly fell in right beside me. As we was headed out a town, ole Sly said, "Can you tell me what you're up to?"

"I just want to go have me a little confab with ole Dick Custer," I said. "I want to make sure that he'll be on the lookout for that Snake Eyed son of a bitch. I could a just sent him a wire message, but I'll feel some better if I talk to the bastard face-to-face."

"I'd feel the same way," Sly said."Besides that, it might be good for you to get out of town for a spell."

"It sure won't hurt nothing," I said. "Hell, ever goddamn time I turn around back there some son of a bitch is trying to kill me."

"Now that we know who to look for," Sly said, "that will likely all come to an end."

"Well, I sure goddamn hope so," I said. "I'm more than just a little bit tired a twisting my neck all over the damn place ever' time I step outside."

We rode on for a spell after that without saying nothing one to the other. We wasn't neither one of us high on small talk, and there wasn't nothing serious to say that hadn't done been said. When we had been out on the road for a good while my throat went to craving some lubrication, and so I pulled a bottle out a my saddlebags and uncorked it. I offered ole Sly a swig, but he politely declined, and so I just commenced to slugging it down my own self.

In a while we stopped to rest the horses, and Sly

brewed hisself up a pot a coffee. I even had a cup of it my own self. Then I went back to drinking my own good brown whiskey. We had just finished up and our horses was rested up plenty. We was about to mount up and head on out when we seed two riders coming toward us from the direction a the county seat. We stood there beside our mounts and waited.

"Do you know them?" Sly said.

"I ain't never seed them before," I said. "You?"

"They're strangers to me."

The strangers come on up close and halted their horses.

"Howdy," said one of them.

"Where you fellers headed?" I asked them.

"Asininity," he said.

"Well, now," I said, "I'm the town marshal a that place, and we been real careful late of any strangers riding through."

The two of them looked at each other real quick-like, and the other one, the one what hadn't yet said nothing, said, "It's Barjack!" They both of them went for their guns fast as rattlers. Sly was faster though. I still swear by God that I ain't never run across no one as fast as that son of a bitch. He hit them both. My bullet hit one of them, but it was the second bullet in the bastard. Sly had done got him. Both of them was knocked plumb out a their saddles. They didn't move none neither. I walked over to them and kicked at them to make damn sure they was dead. They was too. I picked up their sidearms and dropped them in my own saddlebags. Then we flung them both over their saddles and led the horses with their ugly loads on into the county seat with us.

They was unpleasant company. I can tell you that. But we hauled them on in just the same, and when we final come to the county seat, we rid on up in front a ole Dick Custer's office and hitched our horses there. Ole Dick, he must a seen us through the winder on account a he come right out on the sidewalk to greet us personal-like.

"Barjack," he said, "what brings you to town? Other than a couple of carcasses."

"I come to have a talk with you, Dick," I said. "On the way over here we come on these two dumbasses, and they tried to kill me. We got them first. Say, you remember ole Sly here, don't you?"

"Sure," said Dick. "How you doing, Sly?"

"Just fine, Sheriff," Sly said. "How do you do?"

"Doing fine, thanks. Do either one of you know these men?"

"Never seed them before," I told him. "We done talked that over."

"And they just attacked you on the road?"

"Well, you see now, Dick, that there's the reason I come to have a little talk with you. Can we go over to the saloon and find a quiet place to set and talk and have a few drinks?"

Ole Custer hollered at someone to take care a the deceased, and we went on over to the saloon and got us a quiet and kind a private table and set down. I ordered me a tumbler full a good brown whiskey. Ole Dick called for a beer, and Sly just ordered hisself a cup a coffee. Well, the first thing I done was I tuck me a good long drink a that fine stuff. Then I rared back and belched and then I tole ole Dick the whole goddamned story about all the goddamn bastards what had been gunning for me. I wound it all up by telling him what I had found out about ole Snake Eyes. I picked up my glass and had me another long swig.

"We made the mistake, apparently," said Sly, "of

thinking that we were through with hired killers once Snake Eyes had been released from prison."

"Well," ole Dick said, "maybe. Maybe not. Snake Eyes might've contacted these last two before he got out. Maybe they were just slow getting around. Barjack, just what is it you want from me?"

"Dick," I said, "I figger that ole Snake Eyes, he's likely traveling with his little brother what might be calling hisself Jug Marlin or maybe Jug Martin, ole Snake Eyes is likely traveling with him, and I figger they'll have to come through here on their way on into Asininity. I'm hoping that you'll kind a watch out for them and maybe give me a warning that they're on the way."

"You don't want me to arrest them?" Dick said.

"For what?" I said. "We ain't got no proof on them."

"I could hold them for a while on suspicion," he said.

"Then I'd just only have to deal with them later," I said. "No. Just send me a wire over to Asininity, and I'll get my ass ready for them."

I tuck another drink and seed that my glass was empty. I held it up real high for the barkeep to see. He weren't as quick as ole Aubrey to get me some more, but he did get to it eventual. I tuck me another drink.

"I was kinder hoping too," I said, "that you might a heared something over here about them two brothers a hiring guns and such. We're kinder out a the way over there at Asininity, and you might hear something way before I would."

"Well, yes, that's true," he said. "Unfortunately, I ain't heard a damn thing over here. Are you two planning to spend the night here?"

"Sure," I said. "We ain't planning on riding all fucking night long."

"I'll ask around," Dick said. "See if I can find out anything. If I do, I'll let you know before you leave town in the morning."

"I'll damn sure appreciate it, Dick," I said.

Ole Dick got up and started in to leave, but before he tuck on off he looked back down at me.

"If I was you, Barjack," he said, "I'd watch my back. Unless Snake Eyes and his brother are stupid, they wouldn't go up against you to your face, especially if you got Sly here siding you."

Then he walked on out a there, leaving just me and ole Sly setting there together in the saloon. Well, Sly finished his coffee, and I finished up my glass a whiskey, and I waved at the barkeep again. He come over to fill up my glass, and then he asked Sly if he wanted some more coffee. Well, ole Sly surprised the hell out a me by ordering a drink a whiskey. The barkeep went off to fetch it.

"I decided to have a drink with you, Barjack," Sly said. "Just one."

The barkeep brung Sly his drink pretty quick, and me and ole Sly set there a sipping our whiskey. Well, he sipped, and I slugged.

"Hell," I said, "it looks to me like this here might a been a wasted trip."

"Oh, I don't know about that, Barjack," Sly said. "We got those two on the road before they made their way into Asininity. I think we had just about had enough killings there for a while. And Sheriff Custer will surely give us a warning about the approach of the Snake Eyes gang. He might even come up with more information before we leave in the morning."

"Well, yeah," I said. "I reckon you're right about all

that. Ole Dick does keep a pretty damn tight rein on this goddamn town a his. He might could come up with something more."

It tuck a while, but eventual ole Sly finished his whiskey. "I'm going to turn in," he said to me, and he got up to head on over to the hotel. I told him I'd be along in a while. I ordered me another drink, and just about then a little ole saloon gal come a walking over.

"Drinking all by yourself?" she said.

"You can see me here," I said.

"You want some company?" she said.

"Set your ass down here, honey," I said, and she did. She weren't the youngest gal I had saw in quite a while, but she were younger than my ole Bonnie and a hell of a lot skinnier. Well, she weren't exactly skinny. She was all curvy-like in all the right places, you know.

"Buy me a drink?" she said.

"If you'll have a real drink, I will," I said. "I ain't paying no whiskey prices for no glass a colored water."

She kinda giggled, and she said, "I'll have a real drink," so I waved at the barkeep again, and pretty soon the little gal had a drink. I picked it up and sniffed it and even tuck a little sip to make sure it was for real. You see, I knowed, on account a Bonnie's gal business in Asininity, what the score was.

"Okay?" she said.

"Why, sure," I said. "Drink up."

She sipped a little, and then she said, "I don't believe I've seen you around here."

"I don't get my ass over here too much," I said. "I'm the town marshal over to Asininity. Barjack's my name. What do they call you?"

"Poke Salad," she said.

"That's a very interesting name," I said. "Did your mama give it to you?"

She laughed and said, "Not hardly."

"Well, I ain't gonna ask you who it was what did give it to you," I said, and she laughed again.

"You want to take a little tumble, Marshal Barjack?" she said.

We agreed on a price, and I finished my drink, and she tuck me by the hand and went to leading me through the saloon to a back door. Along the way I seed a stranger what seemed to be eyeballing me pretty good, but he didn't make no threatening moves or nothing, so I just kept on a going on. Poke Salad tuck me outside through a back door. There was a cluster a little one-room shacks out back, and she tuck me to one of them. We went inside, and she shut the door. I seed that she never locked it a tall, and in fact, there didn't seem to be no way a locking it.

Poke Salad went to pulling at my coat, but I shoved her off a me. "Just a minute there, Pokey," I said. I tuck the one straight chair in the room and jammed it up under the door handle. It sure as hell wouldn't stop anyone who might be trying to break in, but it would slow him down just a little and make some noise what would warn me. Then I turned around and tuck off my own coat. Poke Salad was stripping herself nekkid, and she did uncover a hell of a sweet little body. Then she tuck to pulling off all a my clothes. Pretty damn soon we got after it, and we had us a time. She done just about ever'thing a gal can do to a man too.

We was just about dressed and ready to leave whenever someone tried to open the door from the outside. Poke Salad yelled out real loud, "Hey! This room is occupied." I had just pulled on my second boot, and I jumped up, grabbed my Merwin and Hulbert, and got my ass over to the door. I jerked the chair out a the way, and pulled open the door, looking out to see who the hell it was. I looked to my right-hand side and seed a bastard hurrying away in the dark. "Hey, you!" I hollered out. He kept on a going, but he looked back over his shoulder, and I could a swore it was the bastard who had eyeballed me in the saloon. Then he was gone.

I just went on back into the little ole shack and finished getting my ass together. I paid little ole Poke Salad. Then I went back into the saloon, but that there suspicious-acting feller wasn't nowhere in sight. I never figgered he would be. I went and had me another drink a whiskey, and then I went on over to the hotel and went to bed.

Whenever I got up in the morning, I met ole Sly down in the lobby, and we went out to find a place to have us a bite to eat. While we was waiting for our food to get cooked, setting and sipping hot coffee, I tole ole Sly about what had happened the night before.

"Would you recognize the man if you were to see him again?" he asked me.

"Hell, yes," I said, "but only I ain't seed him again."

We et our breakfast and had a couple extry cups a coffee, and then we walked on down the street to ole Dick Custer's office. He was in there already, setting behind his desk, and he looked up whenever we come in.

"Morning, Barjack," he said. "Sly."

"Howdy, Dick," I said.

"Good morning, Sheriff," said Sly.

"Snake Eyes is on his way, all right," Custer said. "I found some ole boys who know him. They said he's on the way, but they wouldn't say when, and they wouldn't admit to being tied up with him in any way. I wouldn't be at all surprised, though, if when Snake Eyes shows up in Asininity, he's got at least three men with him."

"Well, by God," I said, "we'll be a waiting for him all right. He'll be damn sorry he ever even thunk about heading back into my town."

Well, just then an ole boy come into the office with some mail for Asininity, and he was a wondering if I would carry it back with me on account a the stage weren't coming through for another couple a days. He had heared I was in town the night before whenever ole Dick was asking around. I said hell yes I'd tote it along with me, and I thumbed through it right then, and I seed that ole Dingle had hisself a piece a mail from New York City.

Chapter Seventeen

Well, we rid the whole way back to Asininity without nothing of no notice happening, and I was by God amazed by that little fact, I was so used to being ambushed and shot at and all, that I was just damn near a missing it. Hell, it was like ole times, I can tell you for sure. It were late at night whenever we got back, and I just went right into the Hooch House. I asked ole Sly to join me, but he just said no on account a he had to get on back home to ole Lillian. I didn't argue none with him, and he went on. I went on inside the Hooch House, and it was doing real good business. It would a did my heart good if I just hadn't a been so all fired et up inside by all the threats to my own person what was taking place at that goddamned time.

Ole Bonnie seed me right off. Never mind about all that crowd and all that noise and all that drunkenness. She never waited for me to make my way over to my table. She come a running at me with her arms out wide to her sides and her big tits a bouncing all over the place, and whenever we come together, she knocked all the wind out a me and like to knocked me over on my ass. I would a fell over except for her arms clamping around me and squeezing me tight and holding me up on my feet. She never turned me a loose, but she did shift around to where we was standing side by side and she just only had one arm around my shoulders, and she walked me back to the table thataway.

Well, ole Happy was there and Butcher and even Dingle was setting there. They all howdied me and swore as to how they was glad to see me back in one piece and all. They asked about ole Sly, and I told them as how he was just fine and dandy and had just gone on home to his little sweetie what had once been mine. Bonnie gouged me in the ribs for that remark. Ole Aubrey had seed me too, and he was right on the spot with my tumbler full a good brown whiskey. I tuck a long swig a that wonderful stuff, and then I leaned back in my chair and pulled a cee-gar out a my pocket. I tuck out a match, but ole Bonnie, she tuck it out a my hand and struck it and held it to the end a my cee-gar. I puffed and puffed and got it going real good. Final I went and told them how me and ole Sly had been jumped out on the road and had kilt us a couple a stupid bastards. Ole Bonnie grabbed me tighter and like to squoze me to death. Whenever I got myself free again, I went and tole them what I had found out from ole Dick Custer, that Snake Eyes and his dumb brother was for sure on the way, most likely with a couple more shitheads, and that would likely show up in three or four days.

"What are we going to do, Barjack?" Happy said.

"Just keep our ass ready for them," I said. "Ole Dick is going to try to spot them over to the county seat and send a wire to warn me when they're on the way, but if they get by his ass, we still have to be ready for them. We can't just depend on ole Dick. No sir. It's my ass they're after."

I had finished off my glass a whiskey by then, and ole Aubrey, he seed it and come over to pour my glass full again. He checked on ever'one else too and tuck care of them. Real casual-like, I reached inside my coat and pulled out the mail and sifted through it 'til I found that there letter for ole Dingle. I held it out in front a my eyes and kind a studied it. Then I tucked the rest a the mail back in my pocket. Ever'one was looking at me.

"Oh, yeah," I said. "I picked up this here mail while I was over at the county seat. This one here what come all the way from New York City is addressed for you, Scribbler."

"For me?"

"Well, now," I said, "who the hell else at this here table is a goddamned scribbler?"

"Good," Dingle said. "From New York. I've been looking for this."

"Now just how the hell do you know you been looking for this?" I said. "You ain't even saw it yet. You don't know who the hell sent it."

"I know all right," he said. "There's only one thing it could be. May I have it?"

I looked at it for another couple a seconds, and I tossed it real casual-like over in front of him. He grabbed it up real fast and ripped it right on open. I never let on that I had been a wanting to do just that thing all the way along that ride back. And I never let on neither that I was damned curious about just what the hell was writ in that piece a communicating. Well, ole Dingle, he read through that thing in a big hurry, and his eyeballs kind a lit up and opened up wide.

"Well, what is it, Dingle?" Bonnie final blurted out.

"It's from my publisher," he said, and then he looked at me. "Our publisher, Barjack. I had written him a letter asking his opinion regarding the book written by the late Mr. Batwing."

"Oh," I said, "writing business, huh? Well, I don't give a shit about that."

"You should, Barjack," Dingle said.

"Shut up and let him talk, Barjack," Bonnie said, and she give me a good hard slap on the shoulder to kind a punctuate her remark. I shut my face.

"Well," ole Dingle went on, "he says that in his opinion, if we get ourselves a good lawyer, we could own all the rights to Batwing's book."

"What's that mean?" Bonnie asked him.

"It means that all the money his publisher paid to him will have to be paid again, and it will have to be paid to us—to me and Barjack. And any money the book makes from here on will come to us as well. I think it could be a significant amount of money."

"Barjack, you might could be rich," Happy said.

"That's wonderful," Bonnie squealed.

"It looks to me like he's rich already," ole Butcher said.

"None of this means a goddamned thing," I said, "if ole Snake Eyes and his boys should come in here and blow my ass away."

You see, the way things was, I just couldn't hardly keep my mind off a Snake Eyes and them. I couldn't help thinking that it was all my own damn fault in a kind a strange way. I'd had a couple a chances when I could easy a killed the son of a bitch, but only I had developed a sort of a soft spot, you might say, for ole Snake Eyes and his damn dumb brother. I had let them go. Oh, I had sent them on off to the pen, but I never kilt them none. Well, by this time, I could almost a kicked my own self in my ass for that goddamned oversight. I sure as hell could, but only I couldn't kick my leg up backward in that way no more. My old age was creeping up on me, you see, and there was some things what I used to could do that I couldn't do no more, and then there was some others that I could still do all right, but only it hurt when I done them.

Ole Lonnie the Geek come in just then, and from the look on his nasty little face, I could tell that he had come into some cash from somewheres. He hustled his ass right on up to the bar and went to slamming his fist on the counter and hollering out for ole Aubrey.

"Just keep your britches on, Lonnie," ole Aubrey said. "I'll be with you in just a minute."

"I got money," Lonnie yelled out, "and I want whiskey now."

"Now, in a minute," said Aubrey. He was used to dealing with that damned Lonnie, and Lonnie sure as hell couldn't ruffle his feathers none. Ole Bonnie, she nuzzled into me then, and when I turned my head to give her a look, she give me one instead, and there weren't no mistaking that look neither.

"You want to go upstairs for just a little bit with me, sweet humps?" I said, knowing right well that was just exact what she was wanting. We got up and made our excuses and headed for the stairs. Lonnie yelled again, and Aubrey brung him a drink and tuck his money. We just kept on along our way, and pretty damn soon we was upstairs and nekkid and in our bed a romping. Now that was one thing what I could still do, and it didn't hurt me none to do it neither. In fact, it felt pretty damn good. Whenever we was did, we had us a drink out a the bottle we kept up there in our room.

"Barjack," Bonnie said, "are you worrying your head about that Snake Eyes guy?"

Well, I tried not to show just how worried I really

was, but I did admit to some worrying about it. "But I got Happy and Butcher and even ole Sly," I said. "I don't see how anyone could have anything more better on his side in a tough situation."

Bonnie snuggled up real tight to me then, and she said, "Oh, I know that, Barjack, but still I can't help worrying for you."

"Now, sweet nipples," I said, "you try not to worry your little ole head."

She pulled me right back down on the bed, and before I knowed what had got a holt a me, we was at it again hard and fast. I tell you what. She like to wore my ass out before she was willing to quit, but I sure weren't sorry about it, not one little bit. Final, we got up and got our clothes back on and tuck our two asses back down the stairs. For once, ole Dingle weren't scribbling. He was reading that goddamn letter again.

"That son of a bitch ain't changed none since you read it last time," I tole him.

He looked up at me with his face a turning kind a red, and he folded up that letter and put it away. Then he went back to his notepad, but he didn't go to scribbling right away. He just only kind a stared at it. I guess the poor son of a bitch was all et up inside with thoughts of all them riches back yonder in New York City. Of a sudden a commotion come from over at the bar, and we all looked over that direction. That goddamn Lonnie the Geek had just throwed a empty bottle at the mirrer behind the bar and smashed it real good, and he was hollering at Aubrey about how he had done spent a small fortune in the Hooch House and he'd ought a be treated better'n that.

Aubrey reached under the bar for the shotgun what he kept there for just such occasions as this here, and Happy and Butcher both of them was up out a their chairs right fast and headed for Lonnie, but just then Lonnie whirled around to face them two, and to my all fired goddamned astonishment, he had come up with a old Remington six-shooter and had the son of a bitch aimed right toward my two depitties. They stopped still, and just about then, I stood up. Being back behind them two kind a stopped me too though. I was trying to figger out what to do to save the situation, when ole Aubrey, being behind Lonnie now, leaned across the bar, turned the butt end of his shotgun around and knocked the shit out a the back side of Lonnie's thick skull. Lonnie dropped like a sack a wet shit.

I strid on over there like as if I had been in control all along, and I said, "Butcher, throw his ass in jail." Butcher heaved the dead-looking Lonnie up over his shoulder and headed out with him. I bent over and picked up the Remington and tossed it on the bar. "Here, Aubrey," I said. He tuck it and stuck it under the bar. He looked at me like as if he was waiting to get his ass chewed out, and I said, "You done good, ole pard." Then I turned to Happy, and I said, "Wonder where ole Lonnie come up with that shooting iron."

"You never give him back his gun, did you?" Happy said.

"No, I never," I said. "It weren't no Remington nohow. That's how come me to be a wondering. Ask around and see what can you find out."

"Yes sir," Happy said, and he commenced to roaming around the room and talking to different folks. I went back to my chair and set back down.

"The dirty little son of a bitch," Bonnie said. "He's ruint my mirrer."

"He sure as hell has did that," I said.

"It'll take forever to get it replaced. That little shit-ass is never coming in here again. He's banned from the Hooch House forever. If he ever sets foot in here again, I'll kill him personal."

"I believe you will, darling," I said, and I damn sure did believe her what she said. She was damn sure hot. She'd been real fond a that there mirrer too. I was thinking that I most likely could get another one over to the county seat, or at least I could order one up from over there, but I never said nothing on account I had just come back from there, and I never wanted Bonnie sending me right on back, not just yet nohow. So I just kept my yap shut. Ole Happy come back just about then.

"Barjack," he said, "no one in here's got no idee where the hell ole Lonnie come up with that gun. Or his money. They're all just about as surprised by it as we was. I'll keep on a checking around though."

"Yeah. Okay. You do that, Happy," I said.

"The little rotten son of a bitch," Bonnie said.

"Who?" said Happy.

"Don't be worrying about it none, Happy," I said. "She ain't talking about you."

"Oh, good."

"I'm talking about that little goddamned bastard Lonnie. Look at my mirrer. Goddamn him to hell."

"Oh," said Happy. "Yeah. He sure busted it up all right."

"Speaking a Lonnie," I said, "hadn't ole Butcher ought to be back here by now?"

"You want me to go check on him, Barjack?" Happy said.

"Go on ahead and do that," I said.

While Happy was heading out, Aubrey brung me

and Bonnie a couple a drinks, and Bonnie thanked him right kindly. I tuck me a big slug out a my tumbler. Well, that was a night a surprises, and I mean that, 'cause just after Happy went out, here come that pettifogging Peester, and he come right over to my table too.

"Barjack," he said.

"Peester," I said, "what the hell brings you over here?"

"I have to talk to you, Barjack," he said.

"So?" I said. "Talk away."

"Uh, privately, please."

"This right here is just as private as it gets, Peester, so either talk or order a drink, or get the hell out of here," I said.

"I understand there have been some attempts on your life since we last spoke," he said.

"Yeah, I reckon you could say that," I told him.

"Well, Barjack, I just want to assure you that I had nothing to do with any of it. I surely don't want anything to happen to you. I hope you believe that."

"Now, Mr. Mayor," I said, "it weren't all that long ago when you was trying like all hell to get rid of me out a here. You was—"

"Barjack," he said, "that was before—"

"Yeah?" I said.

"Well," he said, "you know. That was before."

"Before what?"

Course, I knowed just exact what it was he was talking about. He was meaning to say that he had been ready to get my ass kilt before I told him I had got that little story about him all printed up and ready to be distributed all around the county if any little thing was to happen to me. So now, he didn't want nothing more than to keep me in damn good health. I was just being shitty to the lawyering son of a bitch. He leaned in as close as he could get to me and whispered, but I think ever'one at the table could hear him just the same.

"It was before you had that little tale printed up," he said. "You know what I'm talking about. Everything's different now. I sure don't want you to get yourself hurt. Please believe me."

"Oh, hell, I know that, Peester," I said. "Set yourself down and have a drink."

Aubrey seed what was going on, and he come over to see what His Orneriness the mayor might want to drink, but I broke right on in.

"Aubrey," I said, "bring His Graciousness the mayor of our fine town a drink a my best whiskey in a tumbler just like mine."

"Oh, no, Barjack," Peester said. "I can't—"

"Go on, Aubrey," I said. Aubrey went on, and the mayor set there real nervous-like. Happy come in then, and Butcher was walking along behind him sort a groggy looking. They come back to my table. I looked at them both kind a curious.

"Barjack," said Happy, "Lonnie the Geek is dead."

Chapter Eighteen

Ole Aubrey heared that from clean over to the bar, and he piped up, "I didn't hit him that hard, did I?"

Happy turned toward Aubrey and said, "Oh, no, Aubrey. You never kilt him. Someone stabbed him in the jail cell."

Well, I jumped up then, and I said, "Come on, Happy and Butcher. Let's get our ass over there."

"Where, Barjack?" said Happy.

"Where, hell," I said. "To the marshaling office."

Ole pettifogging Peester got up too, and said, "I think I'd better come along."

"Suit your goddamn self," I said, and I headed for the door with them three right behind me. Dingle grabbed up his notepad and tagged along. We hustled our ass right on over there just about as quick as we could without running. I weren't up to that no more, and when we walked into my office, I seed right off the cell door was standing open. I walked on over there and looked in, and there he was, lying out on the floor with a knife sticking right in his chest and blood all over the floor. He was deader'n hell all right. I turned around to face up to Happy and Butcher.

"All right now," I said, "tell me just what the hell happened here."

"The most I know," said Butcher, "is that I had just

opened the cell door and told that guy to get his ass in there. He was walking in, and somebody come up behind me and sapped me. That's all I remember 'til Happy come slapping me in the face. I come out of it and set up and looked around, and there he was. Just like you see him now."

"Happy?" I said.

"Well, you know, Barjack," he said, "I left out a the Hooch House to come over here and see what was holding up ole Butcher. I found him laid out right there on the floor, and then I seen ole Lonnie lying in the cell with that there knife in his chest. I went to trying to wake up Butcher, and when he come to, me and him come a hustling back here to tell you all about it."

"This is terrible," Peester said.

Dingle was setting down at my desk scribbling like hell.

"It looks as how someone come in behind you, Butcher," I said, "and then sapped your ass and then stabbed poor ole Lonnie the Geek. Who and how come is the questions."

"There is another question," Peester said. "What is 'sapped'?"

"Whopped over the head with a sap," I said.

"A sap?" said Peester.

"It's anything used like a club," Dingle said. "Some kind of a bludgeon."

"Oh," said Peester.

Actual, I hadn't heared that word used that way in a long time, ever since I left New York City, but I never let on.

"So where do you go from here, Marshal Barjack?" Peester asked me.

"Ain't much we can do, Your Horribleness," I

said. "We can just only go around and ask a bunch a questions, is all. And we can commence all that right here and right now. I want each one a you here to take a good look at that there knife and tell me has you ever seed it before."

Ole Peester squinched at it real hard. Then he straightened up and said, "One knife looks like another to me. Sorry, Barjack."

The rest of them all tuck good hard looks, but none of them had no recollections of the damned thing. So I just kind a threw up my hands and said, "Happy, get ole Lonnie tuck care of, and then you and Butcher get to asking all around town and see if you can come across anyone who seed anything or might could know anything what would help us out on this here thing."

"Yes sir, Barjack," Happy said.

"Boss," said Butcher, "I'm just as sorry as I can be that this here happened on my watch, uh, so to speak."

"Don't let that worry you none, Butcher," I said. "Anyone can get his ass sapped from behind."

"Thanks, boss," he said.

Well, I headed back for the Hooch House, and I was some aggravated, I can tell you. I sure as hell had enough troubles of my own without someone sapping one a my depitties and killing one a my prisoners to death right in my own jail cell. For just a bit I tried to figger some way that this here murdering could be connected to ole Snake Eyes trying to get my ass kilt, but there just weren't no way. I got my ass back to my chair and my table in the Hooch House, and ole Aubrey brung me a tumbler a whiskey. Then I had to give Aubrey and Bonnie a whole damn rundown on what it was I had found in my jail cell.

"But who done it?" Bonnie asked me.

"Hell," I said, "I don't know. How could I know? Someone sapped ole Butcher from behind and stabbed ole Lonnie in the chest and then beat it the hell out a there. Far as I can tell, no one seed nothing. The killer's long gone. That's all."

"Barjack?" said Aubrey.

"Whut?"

"What does 'sapped' mean?"

I sighed real long, leaned back my head, and rolled my eyeballs around. "Don't no one in this town understand the queen's goddamned English?" I said, kind a moaning. Then I looked at Aubrey and said, "It means conked on the goddamn head. That's what the hell it means."

"Oh," Aubrey said, and then someone over at the bar starting in to yelling for service, so ole Aubrey hustled his ass back over there.

"Sapped?" said Bonnie. "I ain't never heard that word before neither. Sapped."

"Well, now," I said, "that's on account a you lived all your lone life out here in the goddamn wilderness, and you ain't never even visited real civilization."

Ole Herman Sly come in just then and come on over to join us. He set down and called for a cup a coffee, and Aubrey brung it pretty quick. Sly tuck a sip, and then he said that he had done heared about the killing in the jail cell. Word sure as hell does travel fast around Asininity.

"As if I ain't got trouble enough," I said.

"Do you have any suspicions?" he said.

"Nary," I said.

"There's no way it could be connected to this Snake Eyes trouble?" he asked.

"No goddamn way I can see," I said.

"Can you think of any reason anyone might want Lonnie dead?"

"None in particular," I said. "Just about anyone who was around when he was drunk, including me. After he crashed her mirrer, ole Bonnie sure as hell wanted him kilt, but she was in here whenever he bought the farm."

"Why in the world would anyone want to kill Lonnie the Geek?" Sly said. "He was nothing but the town drunk. The killing was calculated and deliberate."

"Ole Lonnie had got hisself a Remington revolver somewhere too," I said.

Sly give me a curious look.

"That's right," I said. "Whenever he broke ole Bonnie's mirrer, and Butcher and Happy went after his ass, he turned on them with that there Remington. That's when Aubrey smacked him with that shotgun butt, and then Butcher hauled his ass off to put him in a jail cell."

Happy and Butcher come in then and come on over to the table. Happy had something wrapped up in a bandanna.

"What's that?" I asked him.

He laid it on the table and unwrapped it. "It's that knife, Barjack," he said.

"That there's the killing weapon," I said to Sly. He reached over and picked it up to study on it a bit.

"Barjack?" said Happy.

"Whut?" I said.

"Barjack," he said, reaching into his pocket and pulling out some bills, what he dropped on the table in front a me, "ole Lonnie had fifty dollars on him. I don't believe ole Lonnie had ever seen fifty dollars at one time in his whole life."

I picked up them bills and counted through them. It was fifty bucks all right. I tossed them back down and scratched my head.

"We been asking folks out on the street," Happy said, "but no one knows nothing."

"No one seen nothing neither," said Butcher.

"We figgered we could question ever'one in here," Happy said.

"Well, get after it," I said. They started to go, but I said real quick, "Wait a minute." They stopped and looked at me. "Go get that Remington revolver from ole Aubrey," I said. Happy run after it and come back in a minute. He laid it on the table in front a me. "It's kind a unusual, ain't it?" I said.

Sly reached for it and picked it up. "A forty-four," he said. "Eighteen seventy-five model. Frank James carried one like this."

"Take that Remington along with you," I tole Happy. "Show it to ever'one along with the pig-sticker. Ask them if they recognize either one of them things."

Happy tuck up the weapons and him and Butcher started working their way around the Hooch House.

"It's a goddamned puzzle, Sly," I said. "Just where the hell did ole Lonnie come up with that much money and that goddamned forty-four-caliber model eighteen and seventy-five Remington revolver?"

Dingle was scribbling, and Sly said, "If you could figure out the answer to that puzzle, Barjack, you would likely also get the name of his killer."

"I'd just forget about it if it was me," Bonnie said. "The little son of a bitch damn sure and well deserved just what he got. Just look at my mirrer."

"I could just about go along with you on that,

sweet butt," I said, "but some goddamned bastard went and done the dirty deed right smack inside a my marshaling office, and I can't have none a that."

"Barjack is a lawman, Miss Bonnie," Sly said. "He has to put his personal feelings aside when it comes to enforcing the law."

I kind a cleared out my throat, and then I said, "Yeah. That's there's right."

"That's good," ole Dingle muttered, still a scribbling.

"What are you talking about, Scribbler?" I said.

"What Mr. Sly said. 'The marshal had to put his personal feelings aside when it came to enforcing the law.' That's good." Then he looked up at ole Sly and went on, "you don't mind if I use that, do you, Mr. Sly?"

"Feel free, Mr. Dingle," Sly said.

"Oh, shut up, Dingle," I said. "We got more important things on our mind than that just right now."

Dingle kept on a scribbling, and Happy and Butcher come walking back over to the table bringing a feller with them. He was a local feller name a Wayne Doty. I sort a knowed him. He worked a little bitty old farm just outside a town, whenever he felt like working that is.

"Barjack," said Happy, "ole Wayne here might know something."

"Well, does he or don't he?" I said.

"I ain't sure, Barjack, but you had prob'ly ought to listen at him."

I looked up at ole Doty, and I said, "Well?"

"Like I done told your deputies," Doty said, "I seen Lonnie the Geek just yesterday out on the edge of town a talking to a feller, a stranger I hadn't never saw before."

"Has you seed this stranger since then?" I asked him.

"No, I ain't."

"Well, go on then," I said.

"Well, they was down at the livery off to the side a the building, you know, kind a like they didn't want to be seen. I was just riding into town or I wouldn't a seen them either. The stranger, he handed something to Lonnie. I wasn't close enough to see what it was. Lonnie stuck it in his pocket, and then the stranger pulled a gun out from under his coat, and he handed that to Lonnie. Then he said something and then he took off. Lonnie went lurking off toward his house."

"Might that stranger have give Lonnie some cash money?" I asked.

"It might a been," said Doty. "I was too far off to tell."

"And that gun," I said, "could it a been this here Remington?"

Happy still had the Remington, and he helt it out for ole Doty to look at again.

"Like I said, I was too far off to tell, but it could a been all right."

"Could you see a knife in the stranger's belt?" Sly asked.

"I never noticed," said Doty. "I was too far off."

"You done said that," I told him. "We heared you. Can you tell us anything about what this goddamn stranger looked like?"

"Well, not much."

"How much then?" I said.

"Just a little, I guess."

"All right," I said. "Tell it."

I noticed out a the edge a my one eye that ole

Dingle was a scribbling real hard, and I hoped he was scribbling down what Doty was a telling us.

"Well, now, let me see," Doty said. "He was maybe a couple a inches taller than ole Lonnie. It's kind a hard to say on account a he had on a hat, you see."

"What kind of hat?" Sly said interrupting him.

"I'd call it a Montana peak," Doty said.

"Go on then," I said.

"He was wearing a pair a woollies," Doty said. "I noticed them in particular on account a it ain't really woolly weather yet, now is it? I remember thinking he was kind a crazy."

"What else?" I said.

"A striped shirt. A six-gun at his hip. Dark vest."

"Did he have a beard or a mustache?" I asked. "Long hair?"

"I didn't notice none of that."

"What about a mount?" Sly asked.

"Oh, yeah. There was a horse standing a bit behind them. A black, with one white stocking. It was saddled and waiting, so I figure it was the stranger's all right."

"Anything else a tall?" I asked him.

"No. That's all I can recollect."

"That's pretty good, Mr. Doty," Sly said.

"Yeah," I said. "Thanks, Doty."

Doty walked on off headed back for the table what Happy and Butcher had tuck him away from. Happy watched after him for just a bit, and then he said, "What kind of a damn fool wears woollies in this here kind a weather?"

"What's woollies?" Butcher asked.

"Well," said Happy, "they's chaps, but they got wool all over their outside side."

"Oh."

"All right, boys," I said to Happy and Butcher. "See if you can't find this woolly-assed son of a bitch."

Chapter Nineteen

"Barjack," Dingle said. "This publisher owes us a bunch of money."

"You deal with it, Scribbler," I said. I was thinking about that no good son of a bitching stranger in the woollies. I was wondering what the hell he could a been paying ole Lonnie the Geek fifty bucks for and then handing him a Remington revolver on top of that. It just didn't make no sense to me a tall. I had done sent my two fine depitties out to hunt for him, but I didn't have no idee they'd ever find the bastard. He sure as hell weren't hanging around Asininity or else I'd a saw him somewhere or other. He had come into town and found ole Lonnie some way for some reason, paid him off, and give him that there revolver and then tuck off for parts unknown. It puzzled me, and it pissed me off.

"Barjack," Bonnie said, "you'd ought to listen to Dingle. It's a lot of money."

"Hell," I said, "he can take care of it."

"He said they owe it to you."

"Now, listen here, sweet titties," I said, "I got things on my mind. Can't you understand that? Snake Eyes is coming here to blow my ass away. Ain't that enough to keep a feller's mind occupied? And then there's this here new case about ole Lonnie having that cash on him and having that there

Remington shooter and then getting his ass stabbed to death right in my goddamn jailhouse. And my depitty getting sapped in there too."

"How come you keep saying that word, Barjack?" Bonnie asked me.

"Whut?" I said.

"That 'sapped,'" she said.

"Oh, hell," I said, "I don't hardly know how come. I guess ole Butcher just kind a put it back into my head is all. It's a citified kind a word, I s'pose."

"Barjack," said Dingle, "why don't you go back to New York City with me?"

"What kind of crazy fucking thing is that to say to me?" I asked him.

"I just thought that if the two of us—"

"Cut out the thinking and just get back to your scribbling," I said.

It was just only the three of us setting there now, me and Bonnie and Dingle. Sly had left out a little earlier to go back to his Lillian what had used to be my Lillian for a while, and I had sent Butcher and Happy off hunting that woolly. I was feeling like as if there was something what I had ought to be doing about all that shit, but I couldn't figger out just what the hell it might could be. I waved my empty tumbler in the air for Aubrey to see. He seed it and come with the bottle to fill it on back up for me. Then I seed ole Simp coming in waving a piece a paper at me.

"Wire from the county seat, Barjack," he yelled out.

When he come close enough, I grabbed it out a his hand.

"Tell the whole fucking world about it, Simp, why don't you?" I said.

"Well, I just—"

"Oh, shut the hell up," I said. "Go on back to work now."

"I just thought I'd wait and see if you want me to send an answer for you," he said.

"Well, I don't."

"You ain't read it yet," he said.

"I might read the son of a bitch, and I might not," I said. "Either way, it ain't none of your business. Go on now."

"Yes sir," he said, and he turned around and left.

"Hell," I said, out loud but kind a to just my own self, "if I was to have a answer, and if I was to give it to him in here, he'd likely read it out loud to the whole goddamn world."

I unfolded that paper and read it, and then I just tucked it into my pocket.

"Well," said Bonnie, real kind a exasperated, "what is it?"

"It's from ole Dick Custer," I said.

I tuck me a drink a whiskey.

"So what the hell does it say?" Bonnie said. She was getting real for sure fed up with me then, so I decided I better tell her.

"Ole Dick says that Snake Eyes is over yonder in town. His brother and two others is with him. They're drinking around. Don't seem to be in too much of a hurry to kill me."

"Oh, Barjack," she said.

Dingle went to scribbling real fast. He tuck a pause and said, "Barjack, may I see that wire?"

I thunk about making some smart-ass remark, but instead I just pulled the goddamn thing out a my pocket and tossed it over to him. He read it fast and went back to scribbling. Then, without looking up, he handed it back to me and kept scribbling. Then Sly come walking in and come over to the table and set down.

"Barjack," he said, "did I see the telegrapher come in here?"

"You mean ole Simp?" I said. "Yeah, he come in and give me a wire. Ole Custer, he sent it. He says that Snake Eyes and them is lounging around over there."

"How many?" Sly said.

"Four of them all told," I said.

"Do you have any plans for them?" he asked me.

"I ain't thunk too much about it," I said, "other than to have my depitties all armed and ready and watching for them. Ole Dick said he'd send another wire whenever they left town and headed this way."

"We could do it that way," he said. "Just wait for them here, or we could turn the tables on them."

"How do you mean?" I said.

"We could ride out and lay an ambush for them on the road," he said. "Or we could go on over to the county seat and meet them there. That would really surprise them."

"It might at that," I said. "They'll be figgering that we're just a waiting here for them. I doubt that they'll be dumb enough to just ride in here knowing that we're a waiting. They'd likely try to sneak in some way. If we was to do like you said, that would sure as hell surprise the shit out a them, wouldn't it?"

Dingle's scribbling got even faster, and Happy and Butcher come walking back in. They come over and set down.

"We never found no sign a that woolly feller, Barjack," Happy said.

"No one in town ever even seen him," said Butcher.

"No one except ole Wayne," said Happy, "and he done told us ever'thing he knows."

"Forget about him for now," I said. "I got news, and ole Sly here has got a idee. Now listen close."

"Snake Eyes and three other men are apparently over at the county seat," Sly said. "They don't seem to be in a hurry to get over here. They probably think that Barjack is sweating it out waiting or them. I suggest that we don't wait."

"He suggests," I said, "that we haul our ass right on over there and surprise the shit out of them."

"Go kill them over there?" said Happy.

"I'll go for that," said Butcher, and a big grin spread over his face. "When we going?"

I looked over at Sly, and he said, "I would suggest that we leave early in the morning."

"What if they decides to head this way before then?" I said.

"We'll watch the road ahead carefully," said Sly. "If they head this way before we get to the county seat, we'll take them on the road. What do you say?"

Happy and Butcher looked at me. I said, "Let's do it, by God."

"Let's all meet here in the morning," said Sly. "Sunup. Ready to ride."

He stood up then, tipped his hat to us, and left the place. Bonnie hugged onto my arm real tight and looked into my face. She looked right worried too. I patted her fat forearm, and I said, "Don't you go to worrying now, honeypot. I got the best men in the whole damn country on my side. Ole Happy's been with me for a long time now. There ain't no one better. And Sly is one a the most fearsome killers in the whole, wide West. You recall whenever he first come to town what a ruckus he stirred up? And now I got my ole buddy Butcher here with me too. Butcher Doyle. Ole Butcher's daddy is the head a the Five Points Gang, and they run the whole a goddamn New York City. If you want a be worrying about somebody, worry your little head about ole Snake Eyes. He ain't got long left to breathe in this ole world. I can tell you that."

"Be careful, Barjack," she said. "I don't know what I'd do if anything was to happen to you."

Well, now, that was about the most sweetest thing that old Bonnie had ever said to me in all a them years, and I kind a helt her real close and tight, and I noticed that Dingle was scribbling like hell was on fire, what I guess it is.

Anyhow, I went and tole ole Butcher and ole Happy to pack along two six-guns at least and one rifle a piece. I never was so bold as to tell ole Sly what kind a weapons to pack for trouble, but for my own self, besides my ole Henry rifle and my trusty Merwin and Hulbert, I packed a Colt on my wrong side and a couple a pocket pistols, including the one I had tuck off a ole Butcher that one day. I damn sure meant for us to ready for any damn thing from that Snake Eyes bunch, I mean to tell you.

We gathered up first thing in the morning in front a the Hooch House. I never had to tell Bonnie good-bye that morning. I had did that the night before, on account a it tuck a whole lot to make her get up that early. I had ole Aubrey pack us in some grub on account a it's a long day's ride over to the county seat, and just before we tuck off, I doubled check on both a my depitties weapons. They was well heeled, all right, so the four of us tuck off with sabers a rattling, uh, so to speak. We had not hardly got out a town when we heared someone coming up fast behind us, and we all of us twisted our heads around to see what the hell it was, and here come ole Dingle a racing along on a horse, holding on like hell to keep from falling off and to catch up with us. We waited for him, and when he caught up with us, I give him a real curious look.

"Dingle," I said, "I never would a thunk to see you a straddle of a horse. What the hell—"

"I couldn't take a chance on missing this," he said. "It's going to be the climax of our next book."

"Did you bring along a shooting iron?" I asked him.

"No," he said. "I'm just along as an observer. Kind of like a war correspondent."

Well, I weren't sure just what the hell that meant, but I just reached in my pocket and hauled out ole Butcher's bulldog, and I handed it over to Dingle.

"Stick this in your pocket," I said.

"Barjack," he said, "I—"

"Take the son of a bitch," I snapped at him, and so he tuck it, and he dropped it in his coat pocket. I thunk that the poor little scribbling bastard was about to fall off the horse whenever he turned a loose a the saddle horn to take it, but he never. "Let's go then," I said, and we all started in to riding again. Dingle was leaning forward and holding the saddle horn with both hands. He sure did look uncomfortable, I can tell you. We rid on for a spell without saying nothing, but by and by ole Butcher, he piped up.

"Boss," he said, "when we spot them Snake Eyes guys, what do we do? Just take in killing them?"

"Well," I said, "being as how we'll be out a my town, and the county seat has the county sheriff there, we'll have to kind a watch our step. Course, ole Dick Custer, the sheriff, he knows what's going on. Still yet, I don't think we can just start in to blasting their ass without giving no kind a warning."

"I imagine," Sly said, "that we won't have to worry about that. They'll most likely start shooting as soon as they see us."

"Then we start in shooting them?" Butcher said.

"Then we kill them deader'n a goddamn salted slug," I said.

I looked on over at ole Dingle, and I thunk I could see that he was just a dying to write down some a what we was saying, but he was just tormented on account a he was scared stiff a turning a loose a that there saddle horn even with one hand, especially whenever the horse underneath his ass was a moving.

"There'll be four of them, huh?" Happy said.

"That's what the hell we think," I said, "but I say we best be ready for any goddamn thing."

"That's the best way to look at it," Sly said. "You never know."

Whenever we was just a little better than halfway over to the county seat, we stopped off beside the road there where the crick run close by to rest our ass and our horses' asses. Sly built hisself a little bitty fire to make a pot a coffee, and I dug out the grub Aubrey had put together for us. It was just only bread and cold meat and didn't need no cooking. Dingle hauled his notepad out a his saddlebags and went to scribbling as fast as he could scribble. I tuck out my whiskey bottle and had me a snort or two.

Sly wouldn't have none of it, and neither would Dingle, but Butcher and Happy each of them had a little.

"Barjack?" Happy said.

"Whut?" I answered.

"Whenever we get there," he said, "on over to the county seat, you know, whenever we get there, what are we going to do? I mean, do we split up and go looking for them or what?"

"We stick together," I said. "All of us stick together."

"It might could take a lot longer to find them thataway," he said.

"Barjack's right," said Sly. "Suppose we did split up, and suppose you found the Snake Eyes bunch all together in a saloon or someplace. There's at least four of them and one of you. What chance would you have?"

"Oh. Yeah," said Happy. "I get it."

"You better get it, Happy," I said, "and you too, Butcher. Even you, Dingle. Any one a you runs across them bastards by your own self, you'll be dead as—"

"As a salted slug," Dingle said. And he went to scribbling again. "That's what I forgot to write down. 'Deader'n a salted slug.' Yeah. That's a good one."

"Are you listening to me, Scribbler?" I said.

"Yes," he said. "Of course. We all stick together."

"Barjack?" said Happy.

"Whut now?" I said.

"What if one of them wants to give up?"

"Kill him," I said.

"Unless Dick Custer is watching," Sly added.

Well, we finished off the food I had brung along and all of ole Sly's coffee. Sly put out his fire, and we all got mounted up again and ready to go. I guess all a the questions had been asked and answered, and so we all just rid along quiet like for most a the rest a the way. You know, whenever a bunch a men is going off with a mess a killing in mind, they usual has a tendency to be real quiet-like.

Chapter Twenty

We rid along for about half a the afternoon, and I finished drinking up my whiskey supply. I just throwed that empty bottle off to the side a the road. It landed on a flat rock and busted all to smithereens. We none of us had much of anything to say on account a we had done said it all that morning. Well, really that noon about, whenever we had stopped to rest up and all. We was all just a thinking about the killing what was ahead of us at the county seat, I reckon. We was all of us maybe a wondering would we kill or get our ass kilt. Or maybe a little a both. Anyhow, we was kind of a solemn bunch, and that's for sure.

Well, when we at last come into the county seat, it was for damn sure suppertime, and the sun was beginning to get low in the sky. We all of us kept our eyes opened up for any sign a them Snake Eyes bunch, but we never seed any of them that we knowed of as we was a coming in, so I just said that maybe we had ought to stop at the nearest place to get something to eat. We found us a little place that looked to me to be about greasy enough, so we hitched up in front of it and went on in. It was some crowded inside a there, but I never seed no sign a Snake Eyes nor Jug, and a course, I never knowed who the other two with them was.

We set down at a table, all five of us, and when we

got a chance, we ordered us up a bunch a steaks and taters and biscuits and gravy and coffee. They didn't serve no whiskey in that place, and that kind a aggravated me on account a I was craving some for sure, ever since I had emptied my own bottle way back down the road. I figgered, though, that I could eat up my supper real quick-like and then hustle my ass on over to the nearest saloon. We all of us kept a eyeballing the crowd, special anyone new a coming in. We still never seed any of them. Whenever our food come, I et mine in a hurry. Then I went and paid for all a them suppers. I would get my money back out a ole Peester anyhow, you know, and I tole the rest a the boys that they could find me over at the saloon.

"There's about four of them in town," Happy said. "Which one you going to be in?"

"The clostest one," I said. I headed for the door, but Happy stopped me.

"Barjack," he said, "you said we was all s'posed to stick together."

"You goddamn right," I said, "and I'm glad you remember it, too, so hurry on up and get your asses all over to the saloon before I get myself kilt."

Happy looked kind a puzzled, but I walked on out a there. I stood on the sidewalk out there for just a minute looking up and down the street for the various watering places, and I could see two of them real good from right where I was a standing. I picked out the one that was the most nearest to me, mounted up my ole nag, and rid over there. I hitched up again and went on inside. I wanted my drink a whiskey real bad, but even so, I looked over the crowd real careful-like. I didn't see no Snake Eyed son of a bitch, so I went right on up to the bar.

It tuck a while on account a the place was busy, but the barkeep final come around.

"Whiskey," I said. "Good whiskey. Bring the bottle and a bunch a glasses. I got some friends a coming over here right away."

"How many is a bunch?" the dumb ass said.

"Five'll do," I said. I looked around and spotted a empty table back toward the back a the room. "I'll be right over yonder."

He looked like as if he was kind a put out with me, I figgered on account a I was making him walk all the way back yonder with that bottle and all a them glasses, but I never paid him no mind. I just walked on back to that there table and set my ass down and waited. He come on back pretty damn soon, and I paid him for the bottle. It weren't the best, but it was pretty good whiskey all right. I poured me a glassful right away and drank about half of it down. Then Happy and them come in. They spotted me and come back to set down. All except ole Sly. He had stopped off at the bar to get hisself a cup a coffee. He joined us right after that.

"You seen anyone suspicious-like in here, Barjack?" Happy asked me.

"No, I ain't," I said. "I figger we'll drink up here and then move on to the next saloon."

Dingle had pulled out his pad and was scribbling away. I couldn't figger out what the hell he had to scribble about yet, but I never said nothing about it. Then ole Dick Custer come a walking in. He spotted us right off, likely on account a I was a waving at him, and he come right straight on over to where we was a setting.

"Pull out a chair and set your ass down," I said to

him, and he did. Then I said, "Have a drink a whiskey on me."

"All right," he said. "I will."

There was a glass there just a waiting on him on account a ole Sly hadn't used one, so I poured ole Dick a drink.

"What brings you back to town so soon?" he asked me.

"Well," I said, "we just figgered to bring the fight right on over here to them ole boys, you know. Kind of surprise their ass."

"You mean bring the fight to my town instead of yours," he said.

"Well, now," I said, "I wouldn't a put it like that."

"Sheriff," said Sly, "the advantage is always with the side that has surprise with it. They're planning to sneak into Asininity to surprise Barjack. We decided to surprise them. They won't be expecting to see us over here."

"Well, hell," ole Dick said, "I reckon I can't argue with that none, but just whatever you do, don't start the fight."

"The ole Widdamaker here has done filled us in on that idee, Dick," I said. "We ain't stupid." I glanced over at ole Happy and then I added, "Well, not all of us nohow."

Ole Dick give a nod toward Butcher and said, "Who's this?"

"Oh," I said. "I forgot that you ain't never met my newest depitty. This here is ole Butcher Doyle. Butcher, this is Dick Custer. He's the sheriff of our county here."

I seed Butcher kind a stiffen up at the mention a the sheriff, but then he just nodded a howdy.

"Where you come from, Doyle?" Dick asked.

"New York City," Butcher answered.

"New York City?" ole Dick answered like a echo. "What the hell brought you out here?"

"I come looking for Barjack," Butcher tole him.

"We're ole friends," I said. "You know, I spent my first part a my life in New York City. Me and ole Butcher knowed each other back in them days."

"You're from New York City?" Dick said. "I never knew that."

"Well, now you know," I said. "Dick, I'm glad you come in here. I was fixing to drop over by your office anyhow."

"Yeah?" he said.

"I want to ask you has you seed that Snake Eyes crew around lately. We only just got into town. We et across the street, and then we come in here. We been watching kind a careful-like, and we ain't yet seed nothing of them. Course, we ain't checked out all the rest a the saloons just yet."

"I seen them earlier today," Dick said, "but I ain't seen them lately. I ain't been able to find out where they're staying either. They're not checked in to any of our hotels."

"They couldn't have left town yet," said Sly, "at least, not headed for Asininity. We'd have run into them on the road."

"I've had men watching the road from here to Asininity pretty close," Dick said. "I'd know if they left town headed that way."

"I can't hardly believe they've just give up," I said.

"They might have a camp outside of town," Dick said.

"Well, hell," I said, "I reckon we'll just check over the rest a the town, and if we don't run acrosst them nowhere, then maybe we'll ride out and look for a campsite somewheres close by."

"The best bets," ole Dick said, "would be north of town along the creek there."

"Thanks," Sly said.

Goddamn, but he was a polite-acting son of a bitch. Anyhow, ole Dick made some excuse or other and left us, and we finished up our drinks there and headed out for the next saloon. I weren't a tall sure that my depitties could handle much more whiskey and still be worth a shit in a fight, so all I bought in that second saloon was just a shot all around, except only for ole Sly again. He never even had no coffee that time. We didn't see no Snake Eyes in there neither. We left our horses hitched back there at the first saloon we had went in and just walked our way all over the town. We hit ever' goddamn one a the hooch joints in the whole damn town and never spotted no one we was looking for. I was getting damned pissed off, and that's for sure.

We had made our way right back where we come from and was standing there by our ole nags about to decide to mount up and ride out north a looking for possible campsites whenever old Butcher piped up.

"Hey," he said, "is that woollies?"

"Where?" said Happy.

Butcher pointed down toward the end a the street to the north end, and we all turned our heads in that direction, and there, by God, was a feller in woollies. The rest of him seemed to fit the description ole Doty had give us too. Woolly was crossing the street, and he was just getting to a horse what was hitched at a rail there.

"Come on," I said. "Let's get the son of a bitch."

"Hold on," Sly said. "Don't be in a hurry. Just mount up casually and ride in that direction."

I was in a all-fired hurry to get the bastard, but I knowed better than to conterdict ole Sly. He was the killinest son of a bitch I had ever knowed. So we all just kind a climbed into our saddles and turned our nags to the north and started walking them down that direction.

"I don't want that shithead kilt," I said. "I got some questions what needs to be answered by him."

By that time, ole Woolly was in his saddle, and he was headed out a town to the north. We just rid along casual-like behind him. We was far back enough that he didn't pay no attention to us. He might not a even knowed we was back there.

"Is he the only cowboy in these parts that's got woollies?" Butcher asked.

"He ain't the only one," said Happy, "but there ain't likely no one else woolly enough in the head to be a wearing them yet this time a year."

"Oh," said Butcher.

We got out a town and rid on a ways, and then I seed that Woolly bastard turn his head around. He had seed us final. I weren't the only one what noticed it neither. Sly said, "He's spotted us now."

"So what do we do now?" Happy asked.

"Just keep riding," Sly said. "Let him make the first move."

Well, I was a wondering just what kind a first move the son of a bitch might make. I didn't like this kitty cat and rat game one damn bit. Still I didn't want to go against what ole Sly was a saying. You see, he had kind a tuck charge, and I had let him, on account a I knowed that he knowed better than me how to deal with this manhunting business, even though I had done had my own self plenty of experience a my own at it. I had been a bounty hunter long before I become a lawman, and I had did pretty good at it too, even if I have to say so my own goddamn self.

Ole Woolly, he picked up the pace some, and ole Sly, he did too. Still we kept about the same distance betwixt us. Woolly was looking back over his shoulder a little more often by then too. Then he rounded a curve up in the road ahead, and we lost sight of the bastard. That made me kind a nervous. I sure didn't want to lose the son of a bitch now that we had actual come on to him. I kicked my nag to hurry it up, but Sly slowed me back down again.

"Take it easy, Barjack," he said.

I slowed down again. I was thinking that we wouldn't never get to that there curve in the road, but we final did, and when we rounded it, ole Woolly wasn't nowhere in sight. Well, by God, I was pissed off at ole Sly what had tole me to slow down, and I had slowed down, and now we had sure enough lost that goddamned Woolly.

"Sly," I said. "You—"

"Hush, Barjack," he said, and I hushed my mouth for sure.

Sly had slowed us down to where we was almost just standing still. I looked up and down the sides a the road, and then I knowed what Sly had in his devious, criminal-like mind. There was all kinds a cover on both sides a the road, thick trees and bushes, and not far ahead, hills on our left-hand side, with boulders and brush all over their sides. Right beside the road where we was at was a small kind a clearing, and ole Sly, he said, "Let's stop here and have some coffee."

I looked at him like he was crazy, and I said, "Whut?"

"Trust me, Barjack," he said.

Well, we all dismounted, and Dingle helped Sly gether up some sticks and build a little fire. The rest of us unsaddled our nags, all but Sly, and pretty soon ole Sly had coffee a boiling. I couldn't hardly believe what the hell was going on. We all got us a cup full a coffee. Most of us set down to drink it, but I kept on my feet a pacing around. I lit myself a cee-gar and smoked on it, but I was watching that there road up ahead wondering just where that woolly son of a bitch might could be hiding out. By then I had decided that ole Sly was right, that Woolly had pulled off the road somewhere whenever we had lost sight of him, and he was hiding up there some-wheres a waiting for us.

Happy noticed that Sly's horse was still a wearing his saddle, and he moved over to it to relieve the crit-ter by unsaddling his ass.

"Leave him, Happy," Sly said.

Happy looked kind a funny, but he shrugged and walked away from the horse.

"Sly," I said, "just what the hell are we a doing here?"

"Be patient, Barjack," he said. "Remember what I said about letting the other guy make the first move? He's going to have to do something pretty soon. He sure doesn't want to take on five of us. Just him alone."

"The waiting game, huh?" I said.

"That's about it," Sly said.

"You reckon he's setting somewhere where he can see us?" I asked.

"I imagine so," Sly said.

"What the hell's he waiting for?"

"He's trying to figure out what we're up to," Sly said.

"I'd like to know that my own self," I said, but only I just kind a mumbled it.

"Sooner or later," Sly said, "he'll make some kind of move."

Well, I was about nervied out by that time. I had final got me a look at that goddamned Woolly, and then I had lost him, and then ole Sly had me just a waiting along side a the goddamned road for that Woolly to decide to show his ass again. I weren't a tall sure that he would. Hell, I was thinking, maybe he ain't even hid up yonder a tall. Maybe he's rid way far ahead of us and we don't know it. Maybe he rid off the side a the road and knowed a back way off a that hill and was riding lickety split off acrosst the prairie out yonder somewhere. Maybe—

Just then, by God, Woolly come out a the bushes up yonder on the back a his goddamned nag. He turned north, a course, and he commenced to riding real hard. I reckoned he had saw all our horses unsaddled, all except one a course, and decided that it was a good time to light out. Ole Sly was in his saddle right quick and barreling ass after Woolly.

"Saddle up," I said, and we all commenced to saddling up our mounts, and when we got them saddled up, we hit the trail out after Sly, but we couldn't see hide nor hell of that Woolly nor ole Sly no more a tall by then. They was way out a sight.

Chapter Twenty-one

We come onto the straight a that road, and then of a sudden, there was ole Sly just a setting on his nag in the middle a the road looking up the side a the hill to our left. We slowed down and I come to a stop right beside him. The others all hauled up their ass right behind me with a course ole Dingle bringing his ass up way behind as usuable.

"He went up right there," said Sly.

I looked up and seed a kind of a trail going up that hillside, and then I looked back at ole Sly.

"Well, let's go get the son of a bitch," I said.

"Take it easy, Barjack," he said. "He could be laid up there with a rifle. It's a narrow trail."

"Well, whut—"

"Let's just ride on ahead," said Sly.

Well, I was bumfuzzled by that there last remark. After we had been a looking for that woolly bastard all a that time, and then ole Butcher had spotted him like that, and we had follered the son of a bitch out there on the road and chased his ass up on top a the hill, Sly said let's just ride on. Ride on and leave him. Just like that. I couldn't hardly figger out what the hell was in the bastard's mind. I didn't argue none with him though. I kind a give a shrug, and I just headed my ole nag north and rid on. Sly was riding right beside me, and the rest a the bunch was coming on behind us.

"We're still looking for that campsite," Sly said. Nobody else said nothing, so in a minute, Sly added, "I expect that's where Woolly is headed."

That final made some sense to me. I begun to put it all together, you might say. Sly figgered that ole Woolly, he might a been laid up on that hillside trail with a rifle, and that trail was so narrow that he could a easy picked off at least a couple of us before we could react to his shooting. He just didn't want us to take no chances anyhow, seeing as how it was all-fired likely that Woolly was on his goddamn way to the very camp what we was a looking for in the first damn place. I kind a calmed my self down a little once I had worked that all out in my goddamn brain. We come to a place where the crick was right close to the road, kind a running alongside of it, you know, and since I was in a thinking kind a mode at that time, I figgered that this was the place what ole Custer had tole us about for the best campsites. I started in to say something about it, but ole Sly beat me to the punch.

"Let's all watch carefully from here on," he said. "Their camp could be anywhere along here."

We topped a rise in another minute or two, and then we seed the glow of what just had to be a campfire down below and ahead not too far.

"Right there it is," I said. "And they're all down there unless I miss my goddamn thinking on it."

"All except Woolly," Sly said. "Taking the route he did, he couldn't have gotten here ahead of us."

"Let's ride down on them a blasting," I said.

"Barjack," said Sly, "I don't mean to take over

your posse here, but I think you're still being over-anxious."

"I whut?" I said.

"We don't know who's down there yet," he said. "We do know that Woolly's not there. I suggest that we find us a good location where we can hide ourselves and have a good look at just who is there and maybe wait for Woolly to get here. Then we can take them all at one time."

"All right," I said. "I can't argue with that none, but we best do it right quick-like on account a we ain't going to have no more light pretty damn soon."

Well, we was right lucky then on account that camp was on the right side a the road beside the crick, and just about damn opposite a the camp on the left side a the road, the hillside was still steep, and it was still covered with brush and boulders. Down at the bottom of the hill and right alongside a the road was some thick trees. We moved our horses into them trees as quick and as quiet-like as we ever could, and we tied them there so they'd for sure still be there whenever we come back for them. Then we commenced climbing our ass up the hillside, and we posted ourselfs in various hidey-holes along the way. Ole Sly was down clostest to the bottom, and I weren't far from him. The others was scattered along hither and yon. We settled down to wait.

While we was waiting, though, we had a good chance to look over that campsite, and I could see ole Snake Eyes for damn sure. He was there, and he was pacing around a drinking from a bottle. I squinched my eyes real good, and then I seed ole Jug too. There was two other fellers, and I never recanized them a tall. Some ole boys that Snake Eyes had picked up somewheres along the way, I reckoned. I figgered that ole Sly had recanized them too, on account a I recalled that he had tole me he had knowed Snake Eyes before.

Well, I can tell you, it was sure enough tempting to just start in blasting away at them and kill all their asses while we had the surprise on them. They'd a had a hell of a time fighting back too. We was all out in the dark scattered along that hillside, and they was all clustered around a fire down underneath us. But only we wanted to get that goddamn woolly bastard too, and so the best way to do that and to have it all over with and did for sure and at one time was to do just like ole Sly said and wait. Wait for Woolly to show up.

Now, we must a waited a goddamned hour, and I tell you what, my trigger finger sure was a itching. I was just imagining blasting holes in them assholes down around that fire. I could see it all good and clear in my mind, blood splatters and all, and I sure was a wanting to see it all for real. These bastards had caused me all kinds a hell, mental turmoil and physical danger too. They'd had me worrying and watching twenty-four hours a day for some time now. Hell, before we got it all figgered out, I might could a kilt ole Peester for what they was a doing. I thunk about it too, but ole Sly talked me out a the idee. I was really wanting to plug ole Snake Eyes, the sorry son of a bitch.

Then final here come Woolly a riding in from the north. He had made a big circle to get shut of us, and now he was a coming into the Snake Eyes camp where he had been a headed in the first place. It was dark by this time, and I wouldn't a been able to recanize him so soon if it weren't for his mostly white woollies. But whenever he got down to the camp and clumb down off a his ole nag and walked up into the light from the fire, ever'one could see who it was sure for certain. So now we was ready to commence the killing.

The only thing what I hadn't counted on was ole Sly and his goddamn professional scruples. I should a knowed. You see, I had cranked a shell into the chamber a my ole Henry rifle, and I put it to my shoulder and had just about drawed a bead right smack in the middle a ole Snake Eyes's guts, and that damned Sly, he said, "Barjack! What the hell are you doing?"

"I'm fixing to kill me a snake-eyed bastard," I said.

"No, Barjack," he said. "Don't do it."

I lowered my rifle and give him a look. "What the hell—"

"We can't shoot first," he said. "Remember?"

To tell you the truth, I had plumb put that thought total out a my mind. I was full ready to commit a technical murder on those bastards. I knowed they was planning mine, and I didn't see no sense in playing fair with them. Only thing was, if I wanted help from ole Widdamaker, I would have to. I thunk about ignoring the son of a bitch and blasting Snake Eyes' ass, but then, ole Sly, he just might a gone and tole on me to ole Dick Custer, and if he was to do that, why, hell, my ass could a been setting in the county jail. I sure didn't want that to come about. No sir.

"All right," I said. "Whut then?"

"Follow me," he said, and he went and stood up from behind that boulder where he was hid and started in to walking down the hill. I felt like a goddamn fool, but I got my ass up and follered him. Butcher come on along and so did Happy. I never seed Dingle, but I reckon he come along too, last as usual. We went on down that hill real quiet-like, slow and easy, and then we kind a crept on across the road. When we come on close to that there camp, damn near close enough to spit on Snake Eyes and his crew, Sly helt us up. We was standing there in a kind of a half circle. Their backs was to the crick a course. They didn't have no place to go but straight at us, if they was to want to run, what I never thunk was very likely.

"Snake Eyes," Sly said. "We've got you surrounded. Don't try anything."

Ole Snake Eyes and all a his boys kind a jumped, and their hands went toward their six-guns, but they stopped before they went to pulling them. I don't reckon they could even see us where we was at. They stopped kind a still, and they was squinting their eyes this way and thataway trying to find out who it was who was a talking to them. Snake Eyes final asked.

"Who's that?" he said.

"It's Herman Sly," the Widdamaker said.

"What the hell do you want with me?" Snake Eyes asked him, still squinting around.

"And me, Barjack," I said, hoping like hell that knowing I was out there would make them go for their guns and we could kill them, but it never.

"Barjack?" said Snake Eyes. "You're out of your jurisdiction, ain't you?"

"I never come here to make no arrests," I said.

"I ain't broke no laws," Snake Eyes said.

"And you ain't going to," I said, "on account a you're fixing to be dead before you get a chance."

"You ain't planning to murder us, are you?"

"I never felt like it was no murder to kill a goddamn rat," I said.

"You mean to give us a chance?"

"You all back up to one side of that fire," said Sly, "and we'll come in and stand on the other side."

"That sound fair enough to you?" I added.

Snake Eyes never answered that one. Instead, he and his gang just started into backing real easy-like over to what was our left side a the fire. When they was all lined up real neat-like over there, we started walking in to the light easy-like. Sly was the first one and I was next. Snake Eyes went to grinning when he seed us. Then Butcher showed hisself, and then Happy, and final even ole Dingle stepped into the light.

"Five of you," said Snake Eyes.

"That makes it an even fight," said Sly.

"I heared from all over the place that you was coming to town to kill me," I said. "Now's your goddamn chance."

"Barjack?" said Jug. "Remember me? It's Jug. You come close to taking me in to hang that one time."

"That was my mistake," I said. "I should a went ahead and did it. By the way, what the hell's your last name now?"

"It's still Martin, a course," he said. "How come you to ask that?"

"I just want to know what name to put on your grave marker," I said.

"Snake Eyes," said Woolly, talking to his boss but still eyeballing us, "it looks to me like we got us a Mexican standoff here."

"What do you mean by that?" Snake Eyes said.

"I heard about Herman Sly," Woolly said. "They say he never draws first. That way, he always claims self-defense."

"Yeah," said Snake Eyes. "That's right. "So, Widowmaker, what you going to do if we just don't go for our guns? How you going to handle that little situation? Huh?"

"You'll get tired of waiting before long," Sly said.

"I bet I can make them go for their guns," Butcher said.

"Just stand still, Butcher," said Sly.

"I got more patience than you might think, Widowmaker," Snake Eyes said. "A stretch in prison done that for me." He grinned real wide, and he looked around 'til he spied a kind a flat rock just a little bit behind him. He stepped back, and set down. "Relax, boys," he said to his gang. "We got us a little wait here."

I turned my ass around and propped my rifle up against a tree trunk, and whilst I had my back to them bastards, I slipped out my ole Merwin and Hulbert revolver, and then I went and crossed my arms over my chest, but only my right hand what was holding my Merwin and Hulbert was tucked under my coat. I turned back to where I was a looking them in their faces again.

"You know, Snake Eyes," I said, "I ain't got much patience, and I ain't got the scruples what ole Sly here has got. If I get tired a waiting on you here in another minute or two, I'll just blow your sorry ass away."

"But Sly—"

"Sly ain't in charge a this here expedition," I said. Well, Snake Eyes appeared to be a mite more nervous, and he kind a wiggled his ass on that there flat rock he was a setting on. "Oh, yeah," I said, and I looked at that Woolly son of a bitch. "I'd kind a like to know your name."

"Me?" Woolly said.

"Yeah, you. Ain't I a looking at you? You, you

woolly chaps bastard. What's your goddamn name, if you ain't a feared to tell me?"

"I ain't a skeered to tell you my name," Woolly said. "It's Harley Hatch."

"Hatch," said Happy. "By God."

"How come you to pay off ole Lonnie the Geek and give him a goddamned old Remington revolver?" I said.

"He was just doing a little job for me," Hatch said.

"For you?" I said.

"Well, for us."

"Then I reckon you went and kilt him dead in my jail cell," I said. "Likely whenever you found out what a sorry-ass drunk he was."

Ole Woolly, or Hatch, kind a grinned, but he never answered me that one. I was satisfied though. So was Butcher, I reckon, on account a he blurted out, "It was him what sapped me!"

He just strid right on over there to the other side a the fire and grabbed that Woolly by the shirtfront.

"Ever'one keep still," Snake Eyes said.

Butcher drave a fist into Woolly's gut that doubled Woolly over. Then he bashed a right and then a left into the both sides a Woolly's face.

"Sap me from behind, will you?" he said. Then he swung a ferocious uppercut what come from way low close to the ground, and I'm damn sure must a broke Woolly's jaw. For sure it throwed him over bassack'ards. He landed hard and kind a rolled around and moaned and groaned, and then Butcher went to kicking him in the ribs and stomping on him.

"That's enough, Butcher," Sly said.

Butcher kicked Woolly one more time, I guess for good measure. Then he turned his back on the sorry wretch and started walking back to our side a the fire, but just about when he got his back turned, ole Woolly got hisself up on one elbow and pulled his six-gun with the other hand. He was raising that six-gun up to blast ole Butcher in the back, but Happy seed it, and he drawed his Colt and fired. He kilt that goddamned Woolly, and he fired the first shot, the one what set off the son of a bitching war.

Chapter Twenty-two

Now, it's hard to say just what the hell happened next on account a it seemed as how all at once ever'one was a shooting at someone else. I know for goddamn sure that I never waited for nothing after that first shot was shot. I hauled out my Merwin and Hulbert Company self-extracting revolver and blasted away smack at ole Jug, on account a I never had no clear shot at Snake Eyes, and Jug was standing right straight acrosst from me. I sure as hell wanted to shoot Snake Eyes too, but instead I shot ole Jug. I hit him in the hip with my first shot, and he kind a crumpled up, but he was still a shooting. His shots went wild with him being hipshot that a way, and I shot at him again, but I shot while he was a crumpling up, so my second shot went over his head.

"Goddamn it," I cursed, and I shot a third shot. This one creased his goddamned thick skull, but it never kilt him none. It never even knocked the hat off a his head, but there was blood a trickling down his face. I had just only two more shots in my piece, so I was more carefuller with the next one. I drilled him plumb center, and he fell over on his ugly face. I turned to kill ole Snake Eyes then, but I seed that Sly had done dropped him dead. Butcher and Happy had drilled the rest of them all full a holes. Ole Butcher had been nicked high up on his left arm, but no one else was hurt. Dingle was a standing back with that goddamned English bulldog pistol in his right hand, but I don't believe that he had ever fired a single damn shot from out of it. I never checked, and I never asked him though.

"It's over, Barjack," Sly said.

I was so goddamned relieved that I never said nothing. I just stood there for a minute kind a stunned. I couldn't hardly believe that it was really and for sure over with and did. I had plumb got used to being shot at again ever time I turned around. Final I just said, "Yeah," and I holstered my Merwin and Hulbert. I was still a carrying my Henry rifle in my left hand. I walked over to ole Jug's body, and I rolled him over with the toe a my right boot. The others went and checked the other bodies. I squatted down and went through Jug's pockets and found some pocket change what I went and put in my own pocket, and I tuck up his weapons. When the rest a my outfit seed what I was a doing, they went and done the same with the other carcasses. Them ole boys never had much money on them, but we come up with quite a stash a guns and bullets. Final I said, "Load their stiffs up on their horses, and let's haul their ass on back into the county seat."

Well, the boys done that, and we rounded up our own nags and loaded them down with the extry guns and stuff and headed on into town. I asked ole Butcher how his arm was a doing. Happy had done wrapped a rag around the hurt, and Butcher said he was all right. I knowed there was a doc in the county seat. We might have to wake him up, but then, that was all right with me. When we got into town, we stopped in front a Custer's office, but the place was locked up and dark. I told Happy to go find the doc for Butcher, and the rest of us tied our own horses and the horses what was toting the corpuses delete on their backs to the hitching rail there in front a the office.

"Custer might be in the saloon," Sly said.

"Let's check it," I said, and we walked over to the nearest one. Sure enough, ole Dick was in there a having hisself a drink a whiskey. Me and Sly went over to join him.

"Back already?" he said. "You find them?"

"We kilt them dead," I said. "We got the stiffs down to your office."

Ole Dick tuck hisself a drink a whiskey while I waved at the barkeep.

"Tell me about it," he said.

"They shot first," said Sly, and that was all the telling.

The barkeep come over, and I ordered me a glass a good whiskey. Sly surprised me and ordered hisself a shot a the same. Custer ordered up a refill, and then he changed his mind and said, "Just bring the bottle, Jonesy." Jonesy went to fetch it on over, and Dick looked around the room. He final spotted someone he could pick on and called him over to the table. Then he tole that feller to go fetch the undertaker and have him take care a the corpuses what was over in front a his office, and then to take care a their horses too. The ole boy said, "Yes sir, Sheriff," and then he hurried on out a the saloon. The barkeep come back with the bottle and some glasses, and ole Dick, he went and poured us drinks all around. I was sure enough glad to get it too.

"Well, Barjack," ole Dick said, "I guess your troubles are over. Your problem is solved."

"I reckon so, Dick," I said, and I tuck me a drink a

that good whiskey. "But the problem was for real ole Snake Eyes' problem, not mine. He should ought to have knowed that whenever he decided to take me on, he was in for a hell of a goddamn ride." Sly kind a grinned and tuck hisself a sip a whiskey. Just then Happy and ole Butcher come walking in. They spotted us right off and come over to set, and Dick waved at Jonesy, who fetched over two more glasses. Dick poured them each a drink.

"How's the arm, Butcher?" I asked him.

"Ah, it's just a scratch, boss," he said. "But I killed the son of a bitch that give it to me."

"You sure as hell done that, Butcher," I said. "Hell, you've done turned into a sure enough Wild West gunfighting lawman."

Ole Butcher just kind a beamed, and he leaned way back in his chair all puffed up and grinned real wide and proud-like.

"I just wish I could tell my old man about it," he said. Then he had hisself a drink.

"What do you reckon your old man would think about you turning into a Wild West lawman?" I asked him.

"I don't think he'd mind," Butcher said. "It ain't the same as if I'd have become a New York City cop. Hell, it's like a whole different world from here to back there. I even think he might kind a go for the idea. He reads them dime novels, you know. Why, that's how come me to find you out here. He read that Batwing's book about you, and then he told me about it. Then I went and found Batwing, and he brung me out here."

"You mean Batshit," I said. "So your old man read about me, did he?"

"Yeah, and he liked it too."

"Well, hell," I said, "you just might could wind up in ole Dingle's next book your own self. He's been a scribbling down ever'thing about this goddamn Snake Eyes business what he could get."

"To write a new book about it?" Butcher said.

"Hell, yes," I said. "How do you think your old man would feel about that?"

"Me in a dime novel?" said Butcher.

"It could damn well happen," I said.

"Why, I think he'd be real proud of that," Butcher said.

"Say, Barjack," said Happy.

I looked over at him. "Whut?" I said.

"Where is Dingle?"

I hadn't even thunk about Dingle 'til just only then. I kind a looked around like as if I might spy him in the saloon there somewheres.

"He was with us when we tied up over at Dick's office," ole Sly said.

"Goddamn," I said, "I never even noticed."

"Wull, Barjack," Happy said, "where could he of gone to?"

"Hell, Happy," I said, "how the hell would I know? Don't worry about the little shit. There's all kinds a places to go in a big town like this. Ain't there, Dick?"

Ole Dick, he kind a scratched his head, and then he said, "I don't know, Barjack. There's a couple more saloons. I can't think of much other than that."

"Barjack," said Happy, "don't you think I should ought to go out and hunt for him?"

"Goddamn it, Happy," I said, "I reckon if he'd a wanted us to know where the hell he was a going, he'd a said something to one of us. Maybe he's got a secret life or something over here. I sure as hell don't know."

"Well, I'm just a wondering where he could be," Happy said. "I hope he ain't in no trouble or nothing like that."

"What the hell kind a trouble could he be in?" I said. I was beginning to be just a little bit pissed off with ole Happy. "If it'll make you feel any better about it, go on out and hunt for him."

Happy pushed back his chair and stood up. His face tuck on a real determined-as-hell look. "I just think I'll do that," he said, and he turned to walk out a the place.

"Goddamn," I said, and I picked up my glass and tuck a long drink. I finished it off, and ole Dick, he picked up the bottle and reached over to give me a refill. Butcher was damn near ready for one hisself, but ole Sly was still just a sipping at his. He weren't much of a drinker, and that there is the one only thing I can think of to say bad about ole Sly. He was a hell of a man to have standing beside of you in a for-sure fight, but if you was a wanting to tie on a goddamn good drunk, well, hell, he weren't worth much of a shit for that.

"Barjack," said ole Dick, "I'm going to have to write up a report on the killing of those men. Tell me what happened out there, more than just they shot first."

"Well," I said, taking me another drink to kind a lubercate my throat, "we found them out at their camp, out where you said it would be, and we slipped up on them all right. We was standing them on one side a their fire and us on the other side, and none of us had a gun out. They was a scared to draw on us on account a we had the ole Widdamaker here with us. Then ole Butcher here, I don't recall just how, but he found out that it was that Woolly feller, Hatch, I think his name was, was the one what had sapped him on the head in my own marshaling office and then went and kilt my prisoner, ole Lonnie the Geek, with a knife right there in my own jail cell."

I stopped talking and had myself another drink a that wonderful stuff.

"I had to pound his ass for that," Butcher said.

"That's right," I said, "and he damn sure did too. Still nobody had no gun out. Ole Butcher, he just walked right over to the other side a that camp fire, and he stomped Woolly's ass for him real good. Final, I made him stop. I didn't figger that you'd take it too good, ole Woolly being stomped to death like that. So Butcher quit and was a walking back to our side a the fire, and that Woolly, still on the ground, hauled out his shooter and tuck a shot at Butcher's back, and then Happy drawed his shooter and kilt Woolly."

"So that was the way of it, huh?" said Dick. "All right. Then what?"

"I can't hardly tell you about the rest of it, Dick," I said. "Hell, we was all shooting then. On both sides. I know I kilt ole Jug, and I know that them Snake Eyes bastards all got kilt. The only one a us what got hurt was ole Butcher here."

"Hell, Barjack," Butcher said. "I ain't hurt."

"Well," I said, "he got his arm kind a creased. Then we loaded the leftovers up and come back to town."

Dick looked over at Sly, and Sly shrugged. "That's the way it happened," he said. "The only thing I can add for sure is that I killed Snake Eyes."

"Well, hell," ole Dick said, "I reckon that's enough. I can write up a report on that. Everyone knew that Snake Eyes and his bunch were out to kill you, Barjack. There won't be any problems over this."

He poured drinks all around then, and even ole Sly had final finished up his first one, and he didn't make no protest a tall whenever Dick come round to his glass. He just let ole Dick pour it full again. Happy come back then, and he come on over and set his ass down. Dick poured some whiskey into his glass. Happy just set there real quiet-like for a minute. Final he spoke up.

"I couldn't find him, Barjack," he said.

"Who?" I said.

"Well, Dingle, a course," he said.

"Oh, yeah. Dingle," I said. "Hell, he'll turn up."

"I'd sure as hell feel better if I just knowed where the hell he was at," Happy said.

Dick said, "Happy, if anything bad had happened, someone would've come in here to tell me about it. He's all right."

"Drink your whiskey," I said, "and stop worrying your goddamn head. We're s'posed to be celebrating here. We wiped out the goddamn Snake Eyes bunch. I ain't got to watch over my damn shoulder no more."

"Too bad Bonnie ain't here to celebrate with us," Happy said.

"She'll celebrate a plenty whenever we get back home," I said.

"She's prob'ly worrying about you," he said.

"Women's like that," I said.

I drank down my whiskey and shoved my glass toward ole Dick, and he went ahead and filled it up again. I tuck me another drink right away just to make sure that it was still good, and a course, it was.

"Hey, Barjack," said Happy, and he was a grinning like a damned ole possum. "Look. It's Dingle."

I looked over toward the door, and sure enough, ole Dingle was a coming in and headed right for us.

He was a grinning too, but I didn't have no idee how come. He jerked out a chair and plopped his ass right down, and ole Dick poured him a drink and shoved it at him. Dingle picked it up and tuck a drink.

"Thank you, Sheriff," he said. Then he looked right smack at me. "Barjack," he said, "we can catch a train out of here early in the morning."

"Catch a train for what?" I said.

"To New York City."

"What the hell—"

"We need to go see the publisher of Batshit's book. We need to lay claim to our money. I can get us two tickets—"

"Three," said Butcher.

"Three tickets, and we can leave in the morning."

"To New York City," I said, kind a, you know, musing. Whenever I had left out a New York City all them years ago, I never thunk I would ever go back. I didn't have no reason to go back, and I had all kinds a reasons to stay away. I had stomped Butcher Doyle's ass, and I had ever' reason to believe that if them Five Pointers was ever to get their hands on me, I would be dead as a goddamn mackerel in a fish market. But now with what all had happened here lately, ole Butcher had actual become my friend. I didn't need to hide out from the Five Pointers no more. I thunk about it, and I begun to think that I could actual go back if I was to have ole Butcher along at my side.

"All right, Dingle," I said, "you go on down to the station and get us three tickets. By God, we'll go."

"Yes sir!" he said, and he went running back out a the saloon.

"Barjack," said Happy.

"Yeah, whut?" I said.

"What about Bonnie?"

"Well," I said, "what about her?"

"Well, what do I tell her when I get back over yonder and you ain't with me?"

"Just tell her that Dingle and Butcher has hauled my ass off to New York City to get me a bushel basket full a money what that goddamned crooked publishing fella owes to me. And tell her that I'll see her whenever I get back home. That's what to tell her."

"What if she gets mad at me?"

"Then run like hell."

Ole Sly give a laugh at that, and then it come to me how nice and sweet and silly-assed ole Bonnie got ever when Sly come around with his genteel-like behaviors, and I looked over at him, and he went and got my meaning without me even having to say nothing about it to him. He reached over and patted Happy on the arm, and he said, "Don't worry, Happy. I'll go with you to tell her."

Chapter Twenty-three

Well, ole Sly and ole Happy headed on back to Asininity as late as it was, and ole Dingle went and bought our tickets to New York City. Me and ole Butcher just kept on a drinking whiskey, the two of us, 'til Dingle come back to join us. Dick Custer had done left us a while back. We polished off the bottle ole Dick had bought, and then, much as I hated paying a full price for whiskey whenever I had my own saloon back home, I went and bought another bottle for us. I poured us three drinks, and we commenced to swallering them on down.

"Barjack," said Dingle, "I'm certainly pleased that you finally agreed to make this trip with me. We'll come back home with plenty of money in our pockets."

I had a plenty already, but ever since I had become a big successful businessman, I had become like all the rest a that kind a greedy bastard. I just wanted more, you know. So I was really looking forward to the trip my own self, even though I never let on to ole Dingle about it. I just tuck me a good long drink a whiskey.

"I'm kind a tickled about it myself," Butcher said. "I get to tell my pop all about what I been doing out here. Say, Barjack, maybe you could sign your name on Pop's book for him. He'd like that a lot. I know he would."

"Hell," I said, "I reckon I could do that all right."

"We'll have a hell of a good time in the City, Barjack," said Butcher. "I'll interduce you to my pop and my brothers and cousins. We'll go to the best places to eat and drink whiskey. We'll go around and see all the sights. You been gone from there a long time. The train ride will be fun too. We'll see all kinds a sights along the way."

"Butcher's right, Barjack," Dingle said. "You'll have a good time on this trip all right, and it'll be profitable for us."

"Now you're talking good sense," I said. "The profitableness is the only goddamn reason I'm going along on this fool excursion."

"Ah," Butcher said, "you'll have fun. You'll see."

"He's right," Dingle said. "Not to mention the fact that we will right a great wrong."

"I promise you you'll have fun," Butcher said. "I'll see to it you have fun. Butcher Doyle knows how to show a friend a good time in New York City. You can bet on that, and that's for sure."

"All I want to do is just get to town, take care a business, and then get the hell out again," I said. "That's all. I reckon I can take the time to meet your daddy and sign his book for him, but that's all. I ain't interested in taking no tours."

Just then that little ole Poke Salad spotted me, and she come a hustling her ass right on over to the table where we was a setting and plopped down in a chair right next to me.

"Howdy, Marshal," she said, and she was a smiling like she was right glad to see me once again. Course, my Bonnie was in the whoring business with some gals what worked for her, and I knowed the score all right. I knowed she was just a doing her job was all. But then, it was kind a fun to play along with it.

"Well, now," I said, "looky here who's just showed up. Nice to see you again, sweetness. Will you have a drink a real whiskey with me?"

"I'd be just tickled to have a drink a real whiskey with you again, Mr. Barjack," she said.

I poured her one, and she tuck a drink from out of it, and then I said, thinking kind a like ole Sly, I guess, "Oh, yeah, these here is a couple of my friends. This here is ole Butcher Doyle. He's a longtime friend from New York City, and he's my depitty now too, and this here is ole Dingle. He's a scribbler. He writes books about me."

"Books? Really?" she said. "Say, I think that Mercy Minnie got one of them. I seen it yesterday."

Ole Dingle, he perked up some at that.

"She did?" he said. "Well, I'll be. That's just fine."

Poke Salad turned halfway around in her chair and waved a hand real big and hollered out, "Minnie. Minnie, come over here."

The one she called out to was standing at the bar with a cowboy, and she said something to him and broke away from him to come on over and find out what the hell it was that Poke Salad wanted with her. The cowboy looked like as if he was a bit put out about that. He stood with his elbows on the bar and stared hard after Minnie. She come on over to the table where we was at.

"What do you want, Pokey?" she said.

"You know that book you showed me yesterday?" Poke Salad said.

"Yeah."

"Well, it was wrote about this man right here. This here is Marshal Barjack."

"Really? Marshal Barjack? Well, I'm right proud to meet you. I'm called Mercy Minnie on account a I take mercy on horny men."

"I just bet you do, you merciful thing you," I said.

"Is that book really about you?" she said.

"I reckon so," I said. I jerked a thumb toward ole Dingle. "And this here is the man what writ it. Ole Dingle."

Dingle was still grinning, and he stood up and put out his hand for Minnie to take and shake.

"Pleased to meet you, ma'am," he said.

"Oh, well now," she said, "this is a real genuine pleasure. Two celebrities. Right here amongst us. Well."

She pulled out a chair and set down with us, and I seed that cowboy a coming at us. He was at our table right quick-like.

"Hey," he said. "I had her first."

"I reckon you did," I said.

"She's coming back with me," he said.

"I'll see you later, Billy Boy," Minnie said.

He grabbed her by the arm and went to pulling on her.

"Come on with me," he said.

"Later," she snarled, jerking her arm a loose.

Dingle went and stood up like a goddamn fool.

"She doesn't want to go with you," he said. "Leave her alone."

"You mind your own business," the cowboy said, and he swung a hard right, knocking the shit out a poor silly Dingle. Dingle went sprawling back across the table what was back behind us. Butcher was up right fast, and that poor puncher never knowed what he had got his ass into. Butcher's both fists was a flying. I seed him drive one into the cowboy's gut, and I seed two or three of them smack his face and make the blood fly. Ole Butcher, he was a hell of a scrapper all right. It weren't long before that cowboy was flat on his back a groaning. Dingle was standing up again a rubbing his jaw. Then I seed that cowpuncher reaching for a Colt what he wore at his hip, and I hauled out my Merwin and Hulbert real fast, just almost like ole Sly would a did.

"I wouldn't try that if I was you, Billy Boy," I said. He stopped still. I tole him to go on ahead and get up onto his feet. He done that, but he weren't too steady, and I made him take out his Colt with his wrong hand and toss it onto the table. He done that, and I said that he could get it back from the barkeep whenever he was ready to leave. "And you can count yourself real goddamned lucky too, on account a I could a just as easy a stopped your ass with a bullet 'stead a words."

Well, he staggered off, and then them two gals just went to making over us like as if we had just fit the battle a the OK Corral or something. Then by God ole Minnie, she hollered at another gal, and pretty damn soon we had us each a gal to our own self. We had a few more drinks, and then we let them gals take us all out to them little shacks what was out back, each two of us to a different shack. I just hope them other two boys had them as good a time as what I done. Course I went with Poke Salad again, and Dingle, he went with that Minnie, what I'm sure had plenty a mercy on his ass, and Butcher went off with the third one what Minnie had called over to join up with us.

By and by, a course, we was all did with that there

pleasureableness, and we wound up back in the saloon at our same table where I was compelled to buy us a brand-new fresh bottle a that wonderful brown drinking whiskey. You know, there's folks what calls good drinking whiskey "sipping whiskey," and I reckon that ole Sly might even be one of them, but I just never could go along with that. If it ain't good enough to just drink it on down, then it just ain't worth a shit, and that's all there is to that. Well, me and ole Butcher, we was the first ones back in the saloon, and we was feeling just fine, and then here come ole Dingle, the gals had done gone on after some fresh customers, and Dingle was sort a pissed off about something. I could see that right off. Whenever he set his ass down, I poured him a drink.

"What went wrong out there?" I said.

"Goddamn it," he said.

"Couldn't get it up?" Butcher asked him.

"What?" said Dingle. "Oh. No. Hell, no. Nothing like that."

"Well, what the hell's bothering you then?" I said. I couldn't think a no good reason for a man to come out of a room with a nice little whore all grumpy like the way he was.

"She showed me the book they were talking about," Dingle said. "You know what it was? It was *Barjack, the Gunfighting Marshal* by BATSHIT! That's what the hell it was."

Well, I just couldn't help my self. I went to laughing like hell. I thunk it was goddamned funny. I can tell you that much. Ole Dingle had went and got hisself all puffed up over it, and then it turned out to be that other goddamn book. Final I stopped laughing, and I looked over at Dingle, and I seed that his face was a burning red, and I almost went to laughing out loud again, but I helt my self back that time. I just said, "Well, Scribbler, we'll get our money out a that one too, won't we?"

"You're damn right we will," he said.

It just didn't make a shit to me which one a them goddamn books folks went and paid for, long as they paid for one a the damned things, on account a I was a going to make money on them no matter which one they was a packing. At least, if Dingle was right about it I would. It sure as hell did bother ole Dingle though. Now Butcher, he just studied on something the whole time all this was a going on. Final he spoke up.

"Dingle," he said, "let me understand this. You wrote a book about Barjack. Right?"

"Yes," said Dingle. "Of course I did."

"Then that, uh, Batshit, he went and wrote one too."

"He was capitalizing on my original publication," Dingle said. "He was plagiarizing."

"And the reason you and Barjack are going to the City is to get some money out of his publisher? Right?"

"Not just some money," Dingle said. "We're going after the total rights to that book. All the money it has made and anything it will make in the future. Just as if I had written the book in the first place."

Butcher shuck his head kind a slow, and he said, "Okay. I think I got it now."

Right about then, I had to call for another bottle a whiskey, and the barkeep brung it right on over to us. I poured drinks all around. Well, now, I'll tell you what. I never knowed nobody what could out-drink me a drinking good whiskey, but I was of a sudden feeling just a bit woozy. I drank down another glassful real fast, and then I don't recall nothing more about that particaler night.

The next thing I knowed, I was a waking up, and I was on a goddamned railroad train car what was moving along right fast. I figgered that ole Butcher and ole Dingle had hauled my ass onto that thing. Whenever I come awake, I was a craving a glass a whiskey real bad. I seed ole Butcher across from me a snoring like hell, and then I noticed that Dingle was setting next to me. He was a sleeping too. I gouged him right hard in the ribs to wake him up. He muttered and groaned, and I gouged him again. That time he come awake. He looked at me, and his eyeballs was all bleary and reddish-like.

"Oh," he said. "Barjack. Are you all right?"

"Hell, no," I said. "I need a drink."

"Oh, uh, well," he said, "I think there's a dining car down this way," and he pointed back behind hisself. "I'm sure they have whiskey there."

"Come on," I said, and I kind a heaved my ass up out a that there plush bench I had been deposited on. Damn but I felt heavy too. When I was up on my feet, I reached over and slapped ole Butcher on the shoulder. "Wake up," I said. He come awake and in another minute the three of us was headed for the dining car. Along the way I seed all kinds a folks on that damn train. I seed cowboys and bearded old farts what looked to me like they might could a been miners or even hide hunters or something, and I seed some fine-looking ladies and gents. There was even a lawman with his prisoner handcuffed right to his side. And I seed a couple a Indi'ns too by God.

Final we made it to that there dining car, they called it, and got us set down, and then a feller all spiffied up come round to ask us what we wanted.

We ordered coffee all around, and I called for a big glass a whiskey. I tell you what. That there dining car was ever bit as fancy as Miss Lillian's White Owl Supper Club. Even more fancier, really. Well, we had us our coffee and my whiskey real fast. That waiter fella was damn good at his job. Lillian would a sure enough liked to of had him working in her place. He asked us if we wanted something to eat, and I tole him we would in a little while. He went off and left us. I was needing to get that whiskey a running through my veins before I thunk about any goddamn food to eat.

And that first swaller was sure enough good. It was so good that I tuck me another one right soon afterward. Whenever I got to where I could hold my head up and look around, I seed right off that the only folks in that there dining car was all high toned and fancy-like. A couple of them was a staring at us like as if we didn't hardly belong in there with their posh ass, and I was sure enough glad that at least we each one of us had on a suit. Course, they wasn't fresh cleaned and pressed or nothing, and I reckon we could a used us each one a shave.

I drank down all a my whiskey and felt some better, and then I went to sipping my coffee like a right gentleman. I waved that waiting feller back over and asked him what the hell he had what he could fetch us for breakfast. Well, we had eggs and taters and beefsteak and biscuits and gravy what was all as good as any I ever et, and that waiter fella kept our coffee cups full too. Whenever we was all did with it, we set and had ourselves more coffee, and I went and ordered me another glass a whiskey. I had me some time to be a thinking then, and it come to me that by God I was getting just a little bit excited-like about seeing New York City again.

Final we left that dining car, me with a bottle in my ass pocket, and on our way back to our own place, I seed a gambling gal clipping a hoity-toity passenger out a his bankroll right slick. I seed a young couple a snuggled up real cozy together in a corner a one a the cars. It come to me that you could see any damn thing you might want to see on one a them trains. It sure enough was different from my first trip on a goddamn train whenever I had left New York City whenever I was just a snot-nosed kid, and I had hopped a freight to get my ass out a there. I went to thinking over my whole damn life about where I had been and what I had did over all a them years, and I decided that I had not did bad a tall. I had me a pretty good life, and I figgered that it had been a hell of a lot better than it would a been if I had never left that goddamn City a New York and made my way out West.

Chapter Twenty-four

Now, I ain't going into no detail on the rest a that train ride. All I can say for it is that it's a hell of a lot faster and easier and more comfortable than riding on a goddamn gut-jarring stagecoach or even setting on a horse's back for hours or days. Course, the bestest way to pass the time in a awful situation like that is to just stay all drunked up the whole time, and I sure as hell worked hard at doing just that. As a result a that behavior, I don't really have no proper recollections a that railroading trip. I just know I done it on account a I was back in that goddamn New York City, and I do recollect that pretty damn clear.

It all come back to me and then some. When I was a living there, I never noticed some things on account a they was all I knowed, but after I'd been away for all a them years, I did notice. It was crowded like hell. I kept a running into people on the sidewalks. There wasn't no room to just go where you was wanting to go. They was mobs a coming at you all the goddamn time, and they didn't give a shit for where you was wanting to go. Hell, I don't think they could even see you. I thunk they was trying to just walk right over me or right through me or something like that. The streets was just as bad or maybe even worst, what with all the horses and buggies, and the milk wagons, hansom cabs and hacks.

And it was dirty as hell too. There was trash all over the streets and the sidewalks, and there was even worse than that. And if I don't go into no details regarding that there, I reckon you can figger it all out for your own self. I will just say that the very air you has to breathe in that goddamn place stinks to high heaven, and having been away from it all a them years, I like to of gagged whenever I tuck me a suck of air.

But maybe the walking was the worstest. Soon as we hit them goddamned sidewalks, ole Dingle, what was pretty damned familiar with the City, and ole Butcher, what was a course right at home, tuck off fast, and it tuck ever'thing I had in me to just keep up with them. Pretty soon my hip joints and my legs commenced to hurting me real damn bad. It was right fast when I had done did more walking than I had in the last several years a my life. I never walked nowhere except down the stairs and up the stairs at the Hooch House, and from there to my marshaling office and occasional over to Peester's pettifogging office. Any place any farther off than any a that, I rid a horse to.

Well, it come to me that I just couldn't take no more a that walking, and so I hollered out at Butcher and then at Dingle, but there was a kind a roar over ever'thing all a the time, and they didn't neither one a them ever even hear me. I seed a place what looked to me like you might could get a chair and a table and some whiskey, and so I caught up with ole Butcher by a real monumental effort and slapped him hard on the back. He turned around ready for a fight 'til he seed that it was just only me what had hit him.

"I need to set down and have me a drink a whiskey," I yelled into the side a his head.

He nodded real agreeable-like and grabbed onto ole Dingle, and then he led us into this place what was plumb full and you could hardly even walk through it looking for a place to set down. I figgered it was hopeless, and I would never to get to set down again for the rest a my miserable goddamn life, but then I seed ole Butcher lean across the bar and grab a holt a the barkeep and say something to him, and that barkeep come out from behind the bar and went over to a table and said something, and by God, the table was cleared out in a minute. The barkeep wiped it off and stepped back and offered it to us with a sweep a his arm and a big smile on his face, and we went over there and set my weary ass down. Butcher called for whiskey, and we had it in a minute. I was some relieved, I can tell you, but I couldn't say nothing about it on account a the noise level was just too goddamn high, and nobody couldn't hear me if I was to shout at him.

I begun to think that there wasn't no amount a money what could make this bullshit worth while, and I swore to my own self that if I was to ever get my ass out a this goddamn town and back to my comfy little Asininity, I would never again let myself get enticed into making such a goddamned ill-advised journey again as long as I might live. I drank that whiskey down right fast and shoved my glass toward ole Butcher who had tuck charge a the bottle. He filled me up again.

I guess Butcher or Dingle, one of them, had figgered me out by the time we was rested up some and drunk a few drinks a good whiskey, on account a Butcher got up and went outside, and when he come back in, he said something to Dingle. The two of them got up and motioned for me to foller them.

We went outside and there was a hack a waiting for us. We climbed in and it weren't long before that hack driver had us for real out a the crowds. I seed a part a the City what I had never seed before, even whenever I had been a living there. They was nice fancy houses what even had some space around them, and the streets wasn't crowded, and it weren't noisy no longer. The driver pulled up in front a one a them mansions. Butcher got out and me and Dingle follered him. I never seed him pay for the ride. Come to think of it, I never seed him pay for our whiskey neither.

"Come on," he said. He headed right straight for the front door and pulled it open. A mean-looking son of a bitch stepped in his way, but when he recanized Butcher, he smiled and stepped over out a the way.

"I didn't know you was back," he said. "Welcome home."

"Hi, Knuckles," Butcher said. "Where's Pop?"

"He's in the libary," Knuckles said.

Butcher just waved at us to foller him and headed thataway. I was kind a busy looking around at all a the fancy stuff in the house. We was right away in the libary, and the first thing I seed was I didn't see no books nowhere. I seed a little old man what looked like someone's grandpa a setting behind a great big desk a puffing a cee-gar. He had a glass a something to drink setting in front of him. It looked to me like red wine. He looked up when we come in, and he said in a real weak voice, "Butcher, my boy."

Butcher went over behind the desk and bent down to give his old man a hug. Then he straightened up and made a motion toward me and ole Dingle.

"Pop," he said, "I brought some special friends

from out in the Wild West." The old man looked at us, and I thunk I could see his eyes brighten up some. "This here is Dingle," Butcher went on. "He's the man what wrote that book you like so much."

The old man smiled and kind a half rose up out a his chair and helt his hands out. Dingle stepped up and tuck the old man's hands.

"How do you do, sir," he said. "It's a great honor to meet you."

"You wrote a great book, Mr. Dingle," old man Doyle said, "a masterpiece of American letters. It is I who am honored to make your acquaintance. Please sit down." He helt out his hand toward a chair acrosst the desk from him. Dingle set down in it. "Butcher," old Doyle went on, "get the man a drink. And give him a cigar."

"Yes, Pop," said Butcher, "but first I want to make you acquainted with this other gent here. Pop, this is the real honest to God Marshal Barjack."

By God, I thunk the old boy was going to faint dead away right then and there. His eyes opened wide. His jaw dropped. His hands went up to his heart, and he kind a fell back down in his chair. He stared at me for what seemed to me to be a good long while, but it might a been just a minute or so. Then he opened out his arms wide to his sides and smiled at me. Butcher nudged me around the desk where I was forced into hugging the old fart. He final turned me a loose and made me set down acrosst from him. Butcher found a whiskey bottle and some glasses and poured drinks all around. Whenever the old man seed that we was drinking whiskey, he pushed aside his glass, what I had figgered out by then was for sure wine, and had a glass a whiskey with us. Butcher also give us cee-gars and lit them for us.

Then whilst we set back a puffing, Butcher, back beside his pop again, opened up a desk drawer and come out with two books. He whispered something to his old man that got the old man all lit up all over again, and then he brung them two books to me, and he said, "Would you sign these here for my pop, Barjack?"

"Why, sure thing," I said, and I seed that the one book was the book what Dingle had writ and the other one was the one what that dead Batshit had did. I writ my name real big on both of them. I glanced over at Dingle, and I could see that he was a feeling kind a neglected, but he weren't about to say nothing about it. Not in this place. I handed the books over to him, along with the writing pen what Butcher had give me. Dingle done marvelous in covering up his reaction to that Batshit book. He signed the one he had writ and give it all back to me. I give them to Butcher, and Butcher laid them out on the desktop in front a old man Doyle.

Well, now, I don't hardly know how to say it. Old Doyle stared at them two books. He raised up his both hands, but he just helt them up over the books like as if he was a blessing them or some damn thing. He went and picked them up final, and then, I swear to God, he kissed them, each one. Final he put them back down, and then he used, I imagine, ever bit a strength he had left in his old body to stand up and walk around the desk where he hugged the shit out a me.

I wasn't never so goddamn embarrassed in my whole shitting life, I can tell you for sure, and I was sure for certain glad whenever we final got our ass out a that there fancy goddamn house. I don't mean to give you the impression that I got out a there all that fast though. Oh, no. We had to set and listen to ole Butcher, whilst he tole his ole man about how he had went out to Asininity to kill me, but instead he had saved my life by a killing that damned Batshit, and then how I had made him a depitty. Oh, my, but the old man was happy and proud a that. Then Butcher tole him about all a the gunfighting we had been involved in. Final he said that Dingle was a writing another book and that he was going to be in that one. You'd a thunk that he had just tole the ole man about how the Second Coming of Jesus Christ was just around the goddamn corner or something else about equal earth-shattering.

Anyhow, we left there with the promise a what they called a "guest house" what was out behind their mainest house for how some ever long we was to want to hang around New York City. Well, I guess you know that this was not the way I ever thunk that I would be treated by the Five Pointers if I was to ever get back to the City. I'll even admit that once or twice after we come into the City, I got to wondering was this all a trick of ole Butcher's just to get me back in his territory where he could have me beat to death and dumped in a garbage can or something. I wondered just how the hell I had ever managed to grow up to where I did before I run off from there.

Butcher had us another hack, and he got the address a the place what Dingle wanted to pay a visit to and tole the driver. He driv us back into that horrible downtown mess a noise and traffic and stinking air, but I stiffed myself up and said I could take it. In a bit we hauled up in front of a big downtown building, and whenever we got out a that hack, Butcher tole the driver to just set there and wait for us, and the driver agreed real easy-like. We went inside and up a long flight a stairs. My legs got to hurting me again.

By and by, we come to the right floor, and ole Dingle just opened a door and barged right into a office there. I never paid no attention to what it said on the door. I was too busy a huffing and puffing from the long damn climb. There was a gal a setting at a desk there, and she looked up kind a startled-like.

"May I help you?" she asked.

"I want to see Mr. Snot," Dingle said.

"Mr. Snod," she said, really punching that there last sound on his name, "is busy right now. Do you have an appointment?"

"Hell with an appointment," Dingle said, and he headed for the door to Snot's office and barged on in there. Ole Snot looked up, and was for damn sure startled.

"What's this?" he said.

The gal from the outside office follered us in, and she said, "Mr. Snod, I'm sorry. They wouldn't listen to me."

"That's all right, Miss Griez," he said. Then to Dingle what was out front of us, he said, "Who are you, and what do you want here?"

"I'm Dingle, Mr. Snot, and I've come to inform you that you owe me a considerable sum of money."

"What the hell are you talking about? I don't even know you."

"I'm the author of the original Barjack book," Dingle said. "You published a plagiarized version of my book written by Mr. Batshit."

"You mean Batwing's book?" Snot said.

"That's what I just said. By rights, I own that book, along with Marshal Barjack here. You owe me all the money you have paid to Batshit and all the rights to that book, and I'm here to demand that you sign a letter of agreement to that effect along with a check for the amount of money earned to date."

"Mr., uh, I'm sorry, what was your name?"

"Dingle!"

"Mr. Dingle, I don't know what you're talking about, and I'm going to have to ask you to leave this office."

"Very well," said Dingle. "I've given you a chance to settle this without legal action. The next time you hear from me, it will be through my attorney."

Well, we stormed out a there the same way we had stormed in, and we went back down them goddamned stairs and clumb back in our waiting hack. Butcher give the driver a address, and we driv through them crowded streets again 'til we come to a smallish storefront-looking place without no identifying sign on it nowhere. Butcher tole the driver and me and Dingle to wait for him, and he went inside. Pretty soon he come out again and had us driv to another saloon. We went in there and got ourselfs set down more or less the same way how we got set down in the first saloon and ordered us some whiskey and then a meal a real fancy stuff. I can't even recall what it was. Maybe I never really knowed in the first place. I et it anyhow.

We hung out there for a while. Then Dingle commenced to fidgeting. He was anxious to get moving.

"We have to go," he said to Butcher. "I need to locate a good attorney."

"Just relax, Dingle," Butcher said. "We'll get it all fixed up."

"But I—"

"Don't worry about it," Butcher said.

Well, we stayed around in that place drinking

whiskey and just killing time 'til damn near five o'clock when all at once ole Butcher got up and told us, "Come along," and tuck us back out to his still-waiting hack. We all got in, and Butcher give some directions, and we was off again. We went right back to that same building, the one what had the publishing place inside, and Butcher had the hack driver haul up on the side a the street right acrosst from the front door where we had went in earlier. I seed a couple a tough-looking bastards kind a just lounging on the sidewalk acrosst the street, and I couldn't be for damn sure, but I thunk that they give ole Butcher a look.

It was right after five o'clock whenever I seed that Miss Grease come out. She went a walking on down the street and disappeared in the crowd. Then here come Snot. He stepped out the front door and turned to his right and had just about got to where there was a little bitty space betwixt his building and the next one, and them two toughs stepped up close behind him and grabbed him by his two arms and hustled his ass in betwixt them two buildings. I couldn't see real good just what the hell was going on, but I could see some fists a flying occasional, and I did hear some smacks and some hollering and loud moans, even over the goddamn street noise. The crowds a folks walking by on the sidewalk done their best to act like as if they never seed nor heared nothing. Dingle give me a worried look.

"Never mind, Scribbler," I said.

"Just sit tight, Dingle," Butcher said.

There was a couple more smacks and then a loud and terrible kind a scream. The two toughs come out a the dark space a straightening up their suit coats. They stopped for a few seconds a looking up and down the street, and then they crossed the street and walked right close by our hack without never looking up at ole Butcher, and as they went by, one a them tossed something down on the sidewalk. They went on and disappeared. We all of us looked down at what that one feller had dropped. I seed right off that it was a bloody ear, fresh cropped off. So did Dingle, I reckon, on account a he like to got sick, but he did manage to hold it back. Ole Butcher, he just kind a looked satisfied, and he told the driver to take us on out a there.

Chapter Twenty-five

Well, none of us never even said a damn word about what had went on there betwixt them two buildings on that day. Ole Butcher, he just went and had us driv on back to his daddy's house, by way of a tailor's place where we each got us a brand-new suit a clothes, and they was fancy, I'll tell you that. Well, we went out to that there guest house where we got ourselfs all cleaned up and shaved and then dressed up in our new duds. We made it back to the mainest house just in time for a big supper, which was spread out on a long table with folks all up one side and down the other. And me, I was set down at the goddamn head a the table, or maybe it was the foot for all I knowed. Anyhow, me and Dingle was treated like as if we was royalty visiting from somewhere over in Europe or some such goddamn thing.

Red wine was served to ever'one around the table except for me and Butcher and old man Doyle, and we all had whiskey, and I reckon that was all in my honor too. I sure enough did appreciate it too, by God. I was interduced to all the folks there as Barjack, the gunfightinest lawman in the whole Wild West, a damn sight above Wild Bill Hickok and ole Wyatt Earp. Whenever all the food was brung out and spread over the table, we had us a meal what was fit for a king too: pheasant, shrimps, lobsters, oysters, beefsteak, taters fixed up right fancy with little bits a green weeds sprinkled all over them, and all kinds a other good stuff. I wished I could a remembered it all and tole ole Lillian about it and how to fix it and all. That would really a made her ole White Owl the best eating place in a hunderd miles in any direction, and that's for damn sure.

Well, I stuffed my gut, and that's the truth a the matter, and I et better that night than I ever done in the whole rest a my life. I also drunk up a considerable amount a pretty damn good whiskey. Whenever old man Doyle final couldn't keep hisself awake no longer and excused hisself to take his ole ass to bed, Butcher got me a full bottle a good whiskey and walked me and ole Dingle out to the guest house. They was two beds out there and glasses and ever'thing what we might need, so he told us good night and went on back to the big house. Well, I drunked up a good part a that new bottle before I passed on out.

I woked up the next morning still in all my new clothes, and I went and splashed some cold water on my face and had me another drink a whiskey just to get myself going good. I seed right away that ole Dingle was some ahead a me. Course, he hadn't drunk near as much whiskey as what I done. In just a few minutes ole Butcher come in and tole us that breakfast was damn near ready, and so we all went back to the big house and et a breakfast that was damn near as impressive as the dinner was the night before. When we was all did with it and had done had us a plenty a coffee, ole Butcher told his daddy that we had some business what had to be tuck care of, and we went out and clumb back up into a hack that was a waiting there for us.

The hack tuck us back downtown, back to that there publishing place, and then the three of us got out and went back into that office. The hack set there a waiting for us. We got back up to that office and found Miss Grease a setting behind her desk. She stood up right quick when she seed us, and she did look a scared.

"Right this way, gentlemen," she said, and she went and opened the door to ole Snot's office and stepped aside for us. Dingle led the way in. Snot stood up. His face looked like all the color had been drained out of it, but there was bruises and scratches here and there around on it, and his one ear was all bandaged up. Or I really should say, the place where his one ear had been was bandaged up.

"Good morning, Mr. Dingle," he said. "Mr. Barjack." Then he looked at Butcher. "Mr. Doyle." He picked up a letter off the top a his desk and held it out toward Dingle. Dingle tuck it and read it. Snot was holding out a check then, and Dingle tuck that too. He folded the letter and tucked it into his pocket. Then he stuck the check in there too.

"Thank you, Mr. Snot," he said.

"There won't be any need for any further legal action, will there, Mr. Dingle?" Snot said.

"No," said Dingle. "This is quite satisfactory."

We went to a bank where Dingle cashed that check and give me a chunk a the money. Then I said that I was ready to head on back home, but ole Butcher, he said that he had to go back to his daddy's house and say good-bye.

"What do you mean?" I said. "You going back to Asininity?"

"Hell, Barjack," he said. "I got me a job, don't I?"

So ole Butcher went back to Asininity with me

and Dingle. I don't need to tell you nothing about the trip back, just only to say that as soon as we got out and away from the City and I was able to see wide-open spaces again and breathe fresh air and not have to fight them city crowds or hear them city noises, I sure did feel a whole bunch better, and I mean that with all kinds of sincereness. I felt even better again whenever we had made it back to the county seat a my county and rented us a buggy to drive back home in. I thunk about riding on horseback, but my two pards wasn't too hot on that idee.

We got back to Asininity all right, and I hauled that rig right up in front a the Hooch House and got out and headed right in there. Aubrey seed me coming and fetched me my tumbler a whiskey right away. Happy was setting at my table, and he jumped his ass up and come to greet me. Butcher and Dingle follered me in, and all of us set down at my table. Then ole Dingle, he had to tell Happy all about how our trip was such a damn successful one, but only he didn't bother with none a the details a how the Five Pointers helped us out. I drunk down my glass a whiskey, and then I said, "Where the hell is ole Bonnie?"

"She's upstairs, Barjack," Happy said.

"Well," I said, pushing my chair back and standing up, "I best go up and let her know that I've got back."

I went to the stairs and started up. I was about halfway up, when Bonnie come to the landing up yonder.

"Barjack!" she said.

She didn't sound too friendly, but I just kept on a climbing, due to my stupidity. When I reached the top a the stairs, Bonnie wound up and knocked the shit out a me, sending me ass over teakettle back downstairs. I rolled over another time or two and then set up looking up at her. She was a flouncing down, coming at me again.

"How come you go to New York City and not take me along?" she said.

"Now, honey britches," I said, "just lookit how you're behaving. I couldn't take you to no civilized place."

"Bullshit," she said.

"Besides," I went on, "it was strictly a business trip. You wouldn't a had no fun a tall."

Just then ole Dingle come to my rescue.

"Miss Bonnie," he said, and he jumped up and run right over by her side, which in her state a mind was a mighty brave thing for him to do. "Miss Bonnie," he went on, "this trip was practically an emergency. It had been delayed too long already by the Snake Eyes gang, and we just had to get on out there. That crooked publisher was about to steal all of our money, and there was no time to lose."

Ole Bonnie, she looked just a bit confused by all that. She looked at Dingle and she looked back at me. Then she looked at him again.

"Well, did you stop them?" she said.

"We sure did, Miss Bonnie," Dingle said. "We got them to sign over all rights to that plagiarized book."

He pulled the letter out of his pocket and unfolded it and showed it to her. She read through it in a hurry, and then whilst he still had her all kind a fuddled, he said, "And we got a check out of them too, for all the money they had already stolen from us."

"How much?" she said.

Dingle leaned over and whispered in her ear, and her eyes opened real wide and her mouth popped open. "Oh," she said, and she hugged ole Dingle and like to of squashed him. Then she looked at me again. "Oh, Barjack," she said, and she come a running to me and picked me up off a the floor and tried to hug me to death too. "Barjack, honey," she said, "did I hurt you?"

I tell you what. I had me more fine feelings for ole Dingle then than I had ever had before.

John D. Nesbitt

"John Nesbitt knows working cowboys and ranch life well enough for you to chew the dirt with his characters."
—*True West*

FIRST TIME IN PRINT!

Will Dryden picked the wrong time to ride onto the Redstone Ranch. He was looking for a job…and a missing man. But one of the Redstone's hands was just found killed, so tensions are riding high and not everyone's eager to welcome a stranger. The more questions Dryden asks, the more twisted everything seems, and the more certain he is that someone's got something to hide. Something worth killing for. Dryden just has to make sure he doesn't catch a bullet before he finds out what's behind all the…

TROUBLE AT THE REDSTONE

ISBN 13: 978-0-8439-6055-6

FIRST TIME IN PRINT!

OUTLAWS

PAUL BAGDON

Spur Award Finalist and Author of
Deserter and *Bronc Man*

Pound Taylor has just escaped from jail—and the hangman's noose—and he's eager to get back on the outlaw trail. For his gang he chooses his former cellmate and the father and brothers of his old partner, Zeb Stone. Pound wants to do things right, with lots of planning and minimum gunplay, but the Stone boys figure they can shoot first and worry about the repercussions later. Sure enough, that's just what they do—and they kill a man in the process. With the law breathing down their necks and the whole gang at one another's throats, Pound can see that hangman's noose getting closer all the time. Unless his friends kill him first!

ISBN 13: 978-0-8439-6073-0
